HOME AT LAST

HOME AT LAST

•

Kim Watters

AVALON BOOKS
NEW YORK

626 4960

To my husband, Bill, and son, Shane,
thanks for all your patience and love while I finally made
our dreams come true.

To my critique buddies,
Carol, Deb, Marion, Sandy & Shelley,
This one's for you!

To Cathy and Judy
Thanks!

And a special thanks to Dr. Weaver and his staff at Squaw
Peak Animal Clinic for their time and knowledge.

Chapter One

"Can you help him, doctor?"

Sarah Churchill cradled the bedraggled mutt's head. The animal lay shaking on the examining table. Tenderly, she pushed the dirty black hair from the dog's eyes, then stroked the matted fur behind his ears. "I didn't mean to hit him—I—he just darted out from behind a parked car and . . ."

"And into your path," the doctor, a Grant M. Morrison according to the tag on the clinic door, finished for her.

"But it was an accident." Unable to read the man's eyes, Sarah stepped back. "It was. Do you actually think I'd harm the dog on purpose?"

Silence stretched between them. It reminded her of the time she took the blame for her foster sister's car

1

accident. Sarah was ready to grab the dog and find another veterinarian who could help her. But in a central California town the size of Greer, which boasted a population of 8,531, she doubted there were many other options.

As he thrust his hand through his hair, his expression softened. "No. I don't think you would."

"Is he hurt?"

"I don't know. Let's take a look, little fella." Dr. Morrison spoke in a low, soothing voice as he returned his attention to the dog. "I'm just going to check you out and see where you hurt, that's all." With kind, probing fingers, he examined the entire length of the small black body.

As the dog thumped his tail against the metal table, a slight smile played at the veterinarian's lips—quite a change from a few moments earlier. Sarah released the breath she'd been holding, and relaxed her fists which had been balled up at her sides.

This man had nothing to do with her past—he probably had no clue how defensive his actions made her. She should give him some slack. He was only trying to help.

With his focus on the dog, Sarah took the opportunity to study him. Tall and lean, he exuded a no-nonsense attitude, but the dark, curly hair brushing past the collar of his lab coat contradicted his otherwise professional appearance.

Her curiosity aroused, she looked around the rest of

the room, wondering if anything else was out of place. Not that she'd know or anything. Her trips to doctors' offices had been limited. Unless it was an absolute necessity, the people who'd taken her in for foster care hadn't given a hoot about her. They just wanted that monthly check from the government. Most of the time she'd been told to tough it out and not to be an inconvenience.

And she hadn't. She'd almost died rather than complain that her side had hurt. It wasn't until she was in the emergency room that they discovered her appendix had burst. That was home number two. Three wasn't much better. But that was all in the past. When she'd turned 18, she'd hit the road and hadn't looked back.

After a few minutes, the vet's smile disappeared, replaced by a perplexed look as he lifted the dog into a standing position and ran his hands across his body again. "You say you hit him?"

"Yes."

"Where? I don't feel any broken bones."

His gaze captured hers. The intensity of his eyes caught her off guard. She'd never seen such a color before—a cross between the evening sky and the dark, forbidden waters of the lake at her fourth foster home.

She inched her way back to the examining table and looked at the bundle of fur which, now that she had a good chance to look at him, resembled a mop, more than a dog.

"I—I—my tire hit him here . . . I think." She caressed the dog's hip. "He squeaked when he hit the ground and didn't move right away. Not until I got turned round. And when he stood up, he started to limp right away."

"Really?" Dr. Morrison looked at her inquisitively.

Sarah squirmed. She stared over his shoulder at a poster of a family and their big, yellow lab selling some brand of dog food. A made-up family—paid to look happy—but they still resembled a family. Sarah imagined the vet's upbringing. He probably had a big, happy family, a permanent bed, and a house full of love and understanding.

Which was great—for him. She knew those places existed, had often dreamed of living in one of them when she was a kid, until reality had set in. But she wasn't jealous of what other people had; it just made her more determined to succeed.

"If you don't mind my asking, how fast were you going?"

"Not very fast. I wasn't pedaling that hard."

Grant wasn't sure he'd heard the young woman right. "Excuse me? Did you say pedaling?" His hands stilled on the puppy's back as he absorbed the information. "You were on a bike?"

"Yes."

Grant glanced at the dog, then returned his full attention on the woman he guessed to be in her mid-20s. A profusion of curly, red hair stuck out from beneath her faded Oakland A's baseball cap. Freckles dusted her cheekbones and the bridge of her upturned nose. And her lips, full with just a hint of gloss, turned down at the corners, making him wonder if she ever smiled.

Not that he had given Sarah Churchill—whose name he'd gleaned from the information sheet she'd filled out—much to smile about with his sour attitude. It wasn't her fault that things had been going wrong for him all day.

"A bike. I see. Then he shouldn't be too badly hurt." He crossed his arms in front of him and gave her a reassuring smile, glad she wasn't the type who drove one of those big sports utility vehicles. This dog might not have been so lucky.

Still, he didn't know why the image of her riding a bike struck him as funny. He coughed to cover the sound of his laughter. Her attire was totally unsuitable. A brown flowing skirt fell almost all the way to her ankles, while a frilly peasant blouse hung loosely from her slight frame.

If he didn't know any better, he'd say it was at least two sizes too big for her, though with the fashions these days, one couldn't tell. The only items that made sense were the stone-washed denim jacket that had seen better days, and the black army-style boots on her feet.

"Good." The woman adjusted her backpack; a look of relief mixed with hesitation flickered across her face as she shifted her weight from one foot to the other.

"Well I'd—I'd—better get going. I'm sure his owners will be happy it's not serious. Thanks."

The mutt whined, bringing Grant's mind back to the task at hand. He continued to inspect the dog, who obviously enjoyed the attention. In a total show of submission, he rolled over on his back, his four paws batting at the air. Grant took a moment to pat his belly, noticing how painfully skinny he was as her words sank in.

Owners? What owners? With a sinking feeling, he realized his day would go from bad to worse if he let Ms. Churchill leave without the dog.

"Wait! Don't go. This dog is most likely a stray." He sighed. Having seen far too many unwanted animals in his short career, he couldn't understand the irresponsible behavior. When would people learn to fix their pets?

"A stray? As in homeless?" A hint of compassion laced her voice, sending a pleasant tremor through Grant. That, and the fact she hadn't bolted out the door made him think that maybe today wouldn't be a total loss after all.

The mutt whimpered as he touched his hind leg. "Yes. And here's the problem." He parted the matted hair, revealing an inch-long gash. "Let me stitch him up, give him some shots, and the two of you will be on your way."

"The two of us?" Sarah stepped back from the table, feeling her stomach tumble to her knees. "I can't keep him. Between my job and school, I don't have the time, the money, or anything to offer a dog."

Sarah remembered the poster again on the far wall; dogs belonged in families—families with a big house and a bigger yard. A single woman, living in a studio apartment with very little furniture, who had a car that didn't work, wasn't the type of person who should own a dog.

Clutching the strap of her backpack like a lifeline, she forced herself to meet the vet's gaze. She could tell by the look on his face, her reaction upset him. It upset her too. Who was she to talk? Being homeless as a human with no place to turn, no warm bed to sleep in, and no set meals was no fun. She should know, she'd tried it more times than she'd care to think about, but she'd made that choice herself. The dog probably had no say in the matter.

An uncomfortable silence lingered as Sarah watched the man thrust a hand through his now unruly hair. Both he and the dog looked like they could use a good brushing, but that was none of her concern. She had to get home and study for her English test.

Grant shoved his hands into the pockets of his lab coat and turned away. This was a part of his profession he hated. To him, dogs and cats were furry humans. Not disposable objects, thrown away on a whim. But that wasn't this young woman's problem. She'd only done what she'd thought best.

Turning to face her again, he sensed a disquiet about

her, a need. His gaze shifted back to the dog, who gave him a forlorn look and a whimper. They both did. An idea sprang into his mind.

"How do you know you don't have a lot to offer our friend here, if you don't try?" He gave the dog a good rub behind his ears. "It's not your fault he's been abandoned, but there aren't many options. The pound won't work because most of the animals that wind up there never make it out alive, and the no-kill shelter across town is full."

No way he could take the dog home. He'd already rescued two dogs, three cats, two rabbits and a pregnant ferret. His townhouse was full.

"Look, Ms. Churchill, just try it for a week. I'll put up some posters and make a few inquiries with my other clients to see if I can find a place for him. But in the meantime, take him home with you. At least he'd be off the streets and safe." If he could convince her to take the pup home, Grant knew he'd never need to make those posters or phone calls.

"I don't know."

She was wavering. He could tell. Unsure, she reached out and began stroking the dog's belly. The pup grunted in contentment, his tail thumping the metal table again. As she continued to stroke him, he licked the back of her hand. A tentative smile graced her lips. "I think he likes me."

Without doubt, the dog had struck a needy core in the woman. By the look of longing on her face, a companion was the perfect solution. Yet it was the surprise in her voice that made him pause. He couldn't imagine anyone not liking Sarah Churchill.

He did. Why, he'd love her if she took the dog home, it would be one less thing to worry about.

He heard Sarah sigh. "He is kind of cute, isn't he? But I don't know the first thing about taking care of him."

"It's not that hard." As if the dog knew she was weakening, the animal flipped over, sat up and began to lick her face. Her expression switched from surprise, to shock, to utter delight. She leaned in and hugged the dog.

"You've got a deal, Dr. Morrison." She extended her hand. Grant was surprised at the firmness of her grip, the softness of her hand, and . . . how well it fit inside his.

"Great. We should have you on the road in a few minutes."

Ten minutes later, the blood drained from Sarah's face. In horror, she stared down at the bill the woman behind the front counter handed her. "How can it be this expensive for some stitches and a couple of shots?"

Sarah glanced down at her new puppy in dismay. His big, brown eyes, covered by wavy, black hair, stared back at her, and his long pink tongue hung out of his mouth. His floppy ears perked up as he cocked his head and his tail wagged enthusiastically.

Then he moved in and nudged her leg underneath her skirt with his cold nose. Sarah bent down to pet him and he licked her face again. Her heart melted She didn't care how much it cost. She'd figure out a way to pay.

"Will that be cash or check?" the matronly woman asked her as she tapped on the keyboard of the computer. "This thing had better work this time," she muttered as she pushed another key, not giving Sarah another look.

Sarah hesitated, thinking about the $40 in her pocket, her grocery list, which now had dog food and accessories added to it, and the rent that was due next week. No way she could pay for this visit and make ends meet. "Um, can I speak to the doctor a second?"

"Certainly." The receptionist turned to speak into the intercom, but not before Sarah noticed the look of disdain, contempt and pity in her eyes. It was starting already. And she'd only been in Greer three months. "Dr. Morrison, Ms. Churchill would like to speak to you."

"Fine. Tell her I'll be out in a minute."

Thirty seconds later, he leaned against the doorjamb to what she assumed was his office. "Yes?"

Sarah glanced around, making sure they were alone. The receptionist had hurried off to the back room. She inhaled sharply. "I can't afford to pay you—"

She choked on the words. She hated the feeling of helplessness, the feeling of dependence, the feeling of incompetence. After she'd left foster care, she swore she'd never feel this way again. And she hadn't. She'd always respected the fact that she could take care of herself. Until the addition of her new friend.

No way would she give the dog up now because of a silly bill. But she wouldn't beg for a reduced fee either; she had her pride.

Dr. Morrison stared at her as he rubbed a thumb across his bottom lip. A look she couldn't quite figure out flashed across his face before he masked it with a half-smile. "My receptionist must have made a mistake. Let me have the bill a second." He leaned over and grabbed it from her hands.

The longer he studied it, the more defensive she became. "I don't have all the money right now, but I can pay part of it now and make payments every week."

He seemed to ignore her statement. "Let's see, if we take this part out here," he ripped a section of paper out, "and this part here," he grabbed another area, "and this part here," he crumpled the last of the bill in his palm, "it looks like you've got no balance."

Sarah clenched her hands into fists; her breathing became shallow. Blood pounded through her veins as she opened her mouth to speak, but no words came out. Free? He wasn't going to charge her? She didn't think so. Nothing in life came free—everything had a price. No way would she be indebted to this man, this complete stranger, no matter how interesting she found him. She had her pride. It didn't matter how much the darned bill cost, she'd cut some classes and work extra shifts at the diner.

"Ms. Churchill, is something wrong?"

"Wrong?" She advanced on him, ready to wipe that questioning grin off his face. "Wrong?" Using her finger as a pointer, she prodded him in the chest. "Of course something's *wrong*. Listen, Dr. Morrison . . ." Sarah jabbed him again. "I didn't say I couldn't pay the bill, I just wanted to know if I could make payments. I don't take handouts. Is that clear?"

"Yes, clear."

"Good. Now march over there and give me another bill. I'll figure a way to pay it off, even if I have to work here to do it."

A thoughtful expression crossed his features as he glanced toward the room where his receptionist had disappeared to earlier. "Fine. You want a job, it's yours. You can start tomorrow."

Sarah backed away, groaning. Her and her big mouth. She didn't have enough time in the day to do what she had to now. How was she going to fit a few hours in at the clinic?

"You're also going to need to get him fixed."

"Fixed?" Her thoughts flew back to the conversation.

"Neutered. Cut. Whatever word you want to call it. You don't want to be responsible for more pups, do you?"

Sarah swallowed and saw dollar signs going 'ka-ching' in her head. "And just how much is *that* going to cost?"

"Since you'll be working here, we can do a trade. See you tomorrow."

Sarah gave in and gave the vet a weak smile. "I get off work at two. I'll be here by two-thirty."

"Fine."

She knelt down and picked up her new friend, along with a starter bag of dog food and temporary leash and collar. "Come on buster, let's get you home."

Grant could have kissed her as she left the clinic, but he didn't. He simply walked to the plate glass window and watched her fit the dog into the woven plastic basket attached to the front of her bike chained up out front. The old-fashioned red girl's bike suited her just fine. She bunched her skirt up around her knees and settled herself on the seat, answering Grant's question as to how she rode the darned thing.

As she struggled to pedal away, he wondered if he should have mentioned how big the puppy would be when he grew older. Probably not. Sarah didn't look like she needed any more surprises right now.

He turned and walked back to his office to catch up on some paperwork but couldn't keep his mind on the task. The vision of a certain redhead kept intruding. The same redhead who'd officially become part of the team until her debt was paid off.

Sarah. Another worker he couldn't really afford. He sighed. Looked like he'd done it again. He'd picked up another stray—a two legged kind this time. When Gillian found out, she'd kill him.

Chapter Two

Sarah struggled to hold on to her newfound pet that evening. She'd named the mutt Rocky, after the man of her dreams—Rocky Balboa. Strong, dedicated, a fighter. He never gave up when he was down and neither would she. Even if she was soaking wet from head to toe.

Obviously, Rocky didn't like baths, and at this moment, Sarah didn't either. She reached up and pulled a wet strand of hair out of her eyes, glad she'd shut the bathroom door before she'd started. If she hadn't, Rocky would have run through her apartment, leaving a trail of water behind him. He'd already jumped out of the tub three times, and what water he hadn't splashed out with each bounce, he'd shaken all over her and the pale beige walls.

The picture on the bottle of shampoo was a lie. The smiling dog sitting calmly in the blue tub had to be a fake, or drugged beyond belief. Maybe she should have asked Dr. Morrison if doggie Valium existed, but then again, she'd had no idea how hard a simple bath could be.

She lunged at Rocky again, determined to get him in the tub if it killed her. Her beloved little monster still stunk to high heaven; no way she'd let him run loose until she washed off every speck of dirt from his cold, damp nose, to the tip of his black, bushy tail. He skittered around the tiny room and settled behind the toilet.

"Come here, Rocky, sweetie." She crawled toward him. "I won't hurt you, honest." Rocky stared at her, panting, his tail thumping against the white, peeling linoleum.

"Okay then, if begging won't do it, maybe a treat will." She reached over and grabbed a liver snack out of the bag she'd added at the last minute to her grocery cart, instead of that bottle of nail polish she'd been coveting.

Sarah dangled what she supposed was some tasty little treat—that's what the label said but she knew now that labels lied—in front of Rocky's face. He licked his chops and stared at her, but he didn't move.

"C'mon boy. Look what I've got." She inched the morsel closer to his nose, praying he'd take it. He looked at her with brown, sad eyes . . . and stayed where he was. "C'mon on, Rocky. I can't have you smelling up my place."

Sarah continued to dangle the liver treat in front of him. "Please? You can sleep with me tonight if you'll just take a silly little bath." The dog squirmed out of his hiding place and grabbed the treat out of her hand.

The doorbell rang, just as she'd managed to grab hold of Rocky's slick hair. Surprised, her grip relaxed just enough for her dog to wiggle his way out of her grasp and bound back out of reach.

"Darn it, this'd better be good, Lorraine." She flung open the bathroom door. "What's it now?"

Sarah yanked the front door open, but it wasn't her friend taking up all the space in her front hallway. It was Dr. Morrison. All six-foot hunk of him. A smile tilted the corners of his mouth, and his hand was raised in mid air, ready to push the doorbell again. Sarah swallowed a groan.

Bathed in dim light from the hallway and her apartment, he looked good. No, better than good. Fantastic. How had she missed his lop-sided grin and incredible dimples, or the way his black wavy hair and twinkling eyes softened his chiseled features?

Great! Sarah straightened her shoulders as her heartbeat accelerated. It was amazing what a lab coat could cover. She blushed. A Greek Adonis, clothed in tight jeans and cream-colored polo shirt stood in her doorway while she stood covered in water and wet dog fur.

Not that it would matter anyway. Someone with Dr.

Morrison's standards wouldn't even give a girl from the wrong side of town a second look. Even if she was trying to change that, she knew better than to expect too much from him, or anyone. She could rely only on herself.

"Hi, Ms. Churchill," Grant greeted her lightly, not sure how Sarah would feel about him dropping in like this.

The woman seemed to get control of her surprise, but her soft, hazel eyes clouded with suspicion. Not that he could blame her since, with the exception of the time in the clinic, they were practically strangers. And strangers didn't usually appear unannounced on your doorstep.

He thought quickly. "I was in the neighborhood delivering some medication to a client and wanted to stop by to see if you needed any help with your new friend. I hope you don't mind?"

There was no delivery and he'd gone several miles out of his way—only to check up on her progress with the dog, he'd told himself. Not only was he feeling a little guilty about pawning the dog off on her this afternoon, but for some unexplained reason, he wanted to see her again and couldn't wait until tomorrow.

His answer seemed to satisfy her. Her guarded expression dissolved into a neutral one. "No, not at all, Dr. Morrison. As you can see, we're getting along fine."

The sarcasm was not lost on him. Grant wondered

if he'd made a mistake by sending the dog home with her, but then remembered the look on her face as she hugged the mutt and decided the answer was no.

"C'mon in." She backed away from the entrance, holding the door for him. "You didn't bring any drugs, did you?"

"Please, call me Grant. Drugs?" So captivated by her face earlier, Grant finally took a good look at Sarah and realized that her purple T-shirt didn't naturally cling to her; her shirt was wet, outlining the lacy details of her bra underneath. Upon closer inspection, he saw huge water spots on her jeans and drops of water still hung from her curly hair that had been casually tied back in a ponytail.

Obviously, she'd been struggling to give Buster a bath and Buster was winning. He could only imagine the clash between them that had resulted in her appearance. Grant couldn't help himself. He laughed.

"What's so funny?" she questioned tartly, staring up at him. Her nostrils flared and her lips thinned. She folded her arms under her chest, which only accented the fullness of her breasts. Apparently, she wasn't as waifish as he'd first thought. Not even close. Her oversized outfit this afternoon had hidden some pretty tantalizing curves. His laughter died.

He rubbed his day's growth of beard with the back of his hand, trying to think of a plausible explanation. Nothing came to mind and from the sparks flying from her hazel eyes, he figured she wouldn't quite appreciate the humor of the situation. "I, er, I'm sorry. I shouldn't have laughed at you or your predicament. A dog's first bath can be rather . . . traumatic for both parties."

She looked at him for a few moments, her expression grim, though her anger had subsided—somewhat. He could still see the muscles twitching in her jaw and the rigid stance of her posture. "Ms. Churchill? Should I leave?"

"No, Dr. Morrison—Grant. Don't go, I'm sorry. I wasn't expecting visitors. And please, call me Sarah."

He liked the way his name rolled off her lips, like a bubbling brook over stones. Soft and inviting, the sound washed over him, relaxing him, yet leaving him breathless and longing for her to repeat his name. The sudden urge to kiss her crossed his mind.

But he wouldn't. He was simply here to check on Sarah's progress with her new pet.

"Okay, Sarah. Can I help?"

Her hesitation didn't surprise him, nor did the wariness of her tone, but her answer did. "Sure. Any ideas you can give me would be great. We aren't seeing eye to eye, or hand to paw right now. C'mon."

He followed her through her one-room apartment and into a tiny space that qualified as a bathroom. Grant realized as soon as he looked inside that it barely accommodated Sarah and the mutt she'd rescued today, much less himself.

Maybe he should offer to wash the dog himself, but

doubted Sarah would allow it. That she had a chip on her shoulder about accepting help was an understatement, he'd learned that this afternoon. He was amazed she'd even let him assist her now. Cautiously, he entered the room. "Well, here's your first problem."

"What?"

"That." He pointed to the partially filled tub. As he leaned over to pull the stopper out, his shoulder grazed hers. A jolt of electricity surged through him. He wondered if he'd electrocute himself if he put his hand in the water. Beneath his breath he muttered a prayer for strength and pulled the plug. "Don't put water in the tub, what you're actually going to do is give him a shower."

"A shower? That's silly. Then why do they call it a bath?"

The way she wrinkled her nose in confusion amused him again, but he held back his laughter. From what he'd already figured out, Sarah didn't have much of a sense of humor and now was not the time to try to get her to lighten up. She had access to gallons of water. The last thing he wanted was to get his new polo shirt drenched by a sudden show of her temper. His chest still ached where she'd poked him earlier at the clinic.

"Your guess is as good as mine." Grant was glad she had the removable kind of showerhead with a hose attached. It would certainly make his job easier. "Good. You remembered to cover his leg," he said approvingly, looking at the plastic bag taped over the shaved spot where he'd sewn up the dog.

That she'd listened to him and had taken direction was a good sign they would work well together. Although, it was a good thing he showed up when he did. If Sarah had managed to get the dog into the water-filled tub, no amount of plastic would have kept the stitches dry.

"First, you get him into the tub . . ." Reaching to the puppy hiding behind the toilet, Grant pulled him out by the scruff of his neck. "Come on, big boy, a little water's not going to hurt you." He settled him into the tub.

Sarah stood there amazed as Rocky just sat in the tub, his pink tongue licking Grant's arm, his tail thumping on the old porcelain bottom. Her wiggling, writhing, bundle of fur practically rolled over and played dead for the doctor. The nerve. It had to be a guy thing, she decided, as she watched him pull the hose from its hook.

"Then you turn the water on . . ."

The instant the whine of water came through the pipes, Rocky flew from the tub and skidded to a stop at Sarah's legs. At least he hadn't ducked behind the toilet again. She scooped up the quaking dog and hugged him tight.

Letting her guard down, she smiled at Grant. She'd never met anyone like him. His apparent concern for her and Rocky left Sarah at odds with her perception of others. It also helped that his sheepish grin, as he leaned against her tub, made him appear more human, more approachable.

"So, about those drugs?" Grant's laughter joined hers as she set Rocky back into the tub. Two grown adults couldn't bathe one twenty-pound pup. She'd had so little to laugh about over the years, to open up now felt strange, in a good way. But she didn't dare dwell on it. "Now listen here, you brute," Sarah murmured, stroking the puppy's head. "You're going to get a bath whether you like it or not, so just cooperate a little."

Her heart melted at the sight of Rocky's sad, brown eyes, and she gave him a quick kiss on his nose. "Remember what I promised you." She held the unhappy dog in the tub as the doctor wet him down, then lathered him with shampoo.

"Okay, fella. This isn't so bad now is it?" Grant's large fingers continued to gently massage the shampoo into the black, curly fur.

Sarah watched, suddenly feeling a sense of discomfort. She couldn't tear her gaze away from his hands. What would it feel like to have him massage and comfort her? Choking on the thought, Sarah drew back. What was wrong with her? She didn't need anyone else to feel secure. She had herself—and Rocky. That was enough.

Without warning, water and soapsuds hit her in the face. Her dog had decided to end his bath. Momentarily stunned, Sarah released her hold and Rocky shot out of the tub and skittered behind the toilet again.

"What do we do now?"

"We try again, of course . . . in a minute." Grant gave her another grin as water dripped down his cheek and soapsuds clung to the tip of his nose.

Sarah reached behind her, grabbed a towel from the rod and dried herself. "Here." Handing the faded blue material to him, she watched as he dabbed the moisture from his forehead, his face, the strong column of his neck.

Her heart skittered a beat at the seemingly innocent, yet intimate gesture. She inhaled sharply. His tangy masculine scent, mingled with the sweet herbal essence of the shampoo and the not-so-pleasant odor of wet dog fur, assaulted her senses. An intense longing blindsided her as attraction sizzled in the air around him.

She wanted this man in her life. And it scared her to death. The last time she'd wanted anything this bad, her world had crashed down around her shoulders. She'd been a child then, now she was an adult. She wouldn't let that happen again.

The bathroom closed in on her. Sarah looked wildly around. She had to leave, to break this feeling. "Could you finish up? I'll get us some drinks." She escaped.

Still puzzled at Sarah's hasty departure, Grant and his newest friend emerged five minutes later. He'd finally managed to convince the dog that taking a bath was his only choice. Too bad Grant had had to join him in the tub to prove his point. So much for his new shirt.

As he'd washed the dog, he'd tried to wash away the effect Sarah had had on him. Her simple smile and her soft laughter when her defenses wavered sent intricate waves of desire through him. The feelings crashed over him, leaving him struggling to catch his breath.

As they did now. Sarah's shirt still clung to her curvy body. He accepted the glass of iced tea and drank it down in one smooth gulp. His thirst had nothing to do with the energy he'd expended washing the dog.

"Thanks for the drink. I'd better get going. Long day tomorrow." Grant set his glass down on the table as a dead quiet sliced through the apartment.

He could have kicked himself for saying those three words, but he hadn't meant them quite as they sounded. It would be a long day, because he'd been kidding himself that he was just interested in the dog. But as his employee, he couldn't—no, make that wouldn't—do anything about it.

"Yes, a long day tomorrow," Sarah spoke stiffly.

He sensed her complete withdrawal, even though she stood not more than three feet from him. "Sarah, it's not—I'm sorry. That didn't come out right."

"That's okay, Dr. Morrison. I understand. See you tomorrow."

Growing up with mostly women, Grant knew when it was time to make a hasty retreat. And now was one of them. As he strode out the door, he almost tripped over the crate-and-paper sack he'd left in the hallway. "I almost forgot. Here." He tried to hand her the sack.

"What's that?" She eyed the package with suspicion.

"It's something for Buster. Come here, boy. Look what I've got for you." The clean dog scampered to him and sat down. Grant leaned down and stroked the soft fur.

"Rocky. His name's Rocky and he doesn't need anything." Her defensiveness didn't surprise him, but the fists at her sides and the haunting expression on her face did. What was wrong with a little gift?

"No, I suppose he doesn't *need* it, but it would look great on him. Better than the temporary ones I gave you at the clinic." Grant sighed and opened the paper sack to pull out a royal blue collar and leash.

He should have known after her reaction over the bill this afternoon that she wouldn't accept anything from him. "If you're uncomfortable with my giving these to you, I can add them on to your tab. It doesn't matter to me."

But it did.

Gillian was waiting for him when he returned home. "What's this I hear about a new employee?" She paced the floor in his study.

Grant followed her movements around the cramped space. Gillian's agitation didn't surprise him. Tired from the day's events, he stretched his arms over his head and stifled a yawn. "Everyone's been after me to take it easier. What's wrong with getting more help?"

His sister paused by the desk. "I'm not against you getting some help, as long as that's all it is. And in this case, I'm not sure."

"You're misjudging the whole situation."

"Am I? I know you, Grant. But we're talking about a woman this time, not a pet. You can't just clean her up, give her a few shots and find a good home for her when you're finished like you've done with the rest of your strays. She's got feelings."

"And I've got feelings too. It's who I am, whether it's a person or pet that needs help." Scooting his chair back, Grant stood and banged his open palms on the desk ready to fight with anyone—even his twin sister—in order to help Sarah. "When you get back from your booking in LA, come meet her. You'll understand."

Chapter Three

Sarah awoke with a jolt as Rocky pressed his cold, wet nose against her face. Glancing at the clock, she groaned—two in the morning. "Go away, Rocky, I'm sleeping." She turned and flopped the pillow over her head. Rocky circled the bed a few times before plopping down beside her with a big sigh. As he nuzzled his snout underneath her arm, a warm, cozy feeling erupted in her. Sarah reached out and stroked his soft, curly fur. "I think I love you, Rocky."

She dozed back to sleep only to awaken minutes before the alarm sounded to the worst smell she'd ever encountered. A cross between rotten eggs and dirty diapers, the aroma assaulted her nostrils. Struggling to sit up because Rocky had his head lying across her chest, she managed to push him aside and get to her feet.

As she staggered across the room, she noticed Rocky had left a present for her. In the early morning light, a pile of brown stuff oozed into the carpet by the front door.

The alarm went OFF, its blaring beep startled her. She bounded toward the bed to turn it off and stepped on a wet spot on the carpet. "No, Rocky!" she moaned, slapping her forehead. "Dumb me. I didn't take you out last night."

Rocky stood, stretched, then jumped at her as she flung herself on the bed and reached to slam the OFF button. He nipped at her hair and pawed at her back, obviously enjoying whatever game he thought they were playing.

"Oh, you beast, you." She turned over, grabbed him and clutched him to her chest. He started whining. Easing her grip, she ruffled the hair behind his ears as she remembered all the diapers she'd changed in home number three. "You're not potty-trained, are you?" She lifted him into the air and bounced him like a baby. "Well, that'll change. Mr. Baxter, my landlord, won't like it if you ruin the carpet."

She set him down, cleaned up the mess, then took him for a quick walk. As she hurriedly dressed for her shift at the diner, she wished she'd listened to Grant's advice and had kept the kennel he'd offered. She should have known after the escapade with the bath that Rocky wasn't going to be easy to handle, but she'd let her pride get in the way. Look where it had gotten her. She'd disappointed her new boss and now had wet, brown spots on her carpet.

Today, Rocky would be stuck in the tiny kitchen behind a makeshift gate while she was gone so he couldn't cause any more trouble, and tonight he'd be in a kennel. What could one of those things cost anyway? She'd just add it on to her already outrageous bill. She leaned down to kiss him good-bye. "Be a good boy, Rocky. I mean it."

Eight hours later, Sarah pedaled like crazy to get to her apartment. She had to let Rocky out, change, and get to the clinic to start working off her debt. She was late.

It wasn't her fault the other waitress, Mabel, had called in sick which left Sarah to do all the work at Greer's diner. And it certainly wasn't her fault the lunch rush lasted longer and stayed later than usual. She glanced at her watch—2:25. She'd never make it, and she couldn't call even if she had the number. She didn't have a phone.

Barreling through the last intersection, Sarah just missed a turning vehicle and skidded to a halt in the complex driveway. She locked up her precious bike, her only means of transportation, and started up the stairs.

On the second level, the resident busybody, Mrs. Maddox, stopped her. "Good afternoon, Sarah." She planted her rotund body in her path and Sarah skidded to a halt, barely stopping in time from plowing into the elderly woman.

"Hi, Mrs. Maddox. Going out? It's a beautiful day." Sarah fidgeted with a loose strand of hair, not wanting to continue the conversation, but not wanting to be rude either. Upstairs, she swore she heard Rocky scratch at the door, which was impossible. He was locked in the kitchen.

"No. Actually, I was waiting for you, my dear. I saw you ride up just now and practically get yourself killed. Why in my day a young woman didn't . . ."

Sarah's stomach clenched, thinking about the upcoming lecture. Mrs. Maddox was at least 80 and living in a time warp. Her downstairs neighbor didn't believe in women working outside the home or living on their own, and wasn't afraid to voice her opinion. Sarah didn't want to think about the speech she'd get if the woman knew of her past.

"Times have changed." She tried to slink by her.

"Yes, yes. So they tell me." She tsked. "Now, there was something else I meant to tell you. What was it?"

Sarah leaned against the dingy white wall, knowing she'd be stuck until her neighbor's memory came back. Everyone in the building knew how scatterbrained Mrs. Maddox was and tried to avoid her. Usually, Sarah was lucky, but today everything was going wrong.

Upstairs, Sarah could definitely hear Rocky's whine. Her poor pet had been locked up too long and probably needed to go to the bathroom, if he hadn't already.

"Oh yes. Seems like a nice fellow. My Harry would have liked him. Why, he took out my garbage last night. Came right down from your floor and swept it out of my arms as he pointed to that Justin Altman's skateboard lying in the hallway. I'm blind in the dark. Why I would've fallen down the stairs if your young man hadn't come to my rescue."

Sarah's jaw dropped open. She had to be talking about Grant. No one besides Lorraine, who lived two doors from Sarah, had ever come to her apartment. Where was the lecture, the chastising about men coming to visit single women? "But, he's not my man, he's just . . ." Just what? An interesting, and kind man, and as far as she was concerned, unavailable. She swallowed. ". . . he's just a friend."

"Oh. What a pity. I suppose you're off again. You young people always are. Can't seem to stay in one place. Well, don't let me stop you. Just make sure you bring your friend by for proper introductions next time he visits."

"Sure." Sarah doubted that would happen any time soon. Relieved, she brushed past her and started up the stairs.

"And as for your other friend, bring him by to visit soon too. I always wanted a dog. But my poor Harry . . ."

Stunned, she nodded, wondering how her neighbor had found out about Rocky. Mrs. Maddox must have heard him downstairs in her apartment. Great! Obviously, Sarah's idea hadn't worked. If Rocky had whined, scratched and barked all day, then the whole building knew about him. Mr. Baxter was sure to visit. She hoped he liked dogs.

Dashing up the remaining stairs, Sarah was glad to finally be home. Home. Something she had little experience with, but after three months in Greer, it started to feel that way. It had to be Rocky. She threw open the door and entered. "Rocky, I'm home."

Her elation died and her heart sank as a black, wiggly body came charging out from behind her futon, a scrap of red fabric, suspiciously looking like one of her favorite pairs of underwear, dangled from his mouth. Sarah groaned and stepped further into her apartment and eyed the entire area in disbelief. Rocky was supposed to be contained in the kitchen, not gnawing on her underwear, or as she looked around, her shoes, her furniture and her schoolbooks.

An earthquake couldn't have done as much damage.

Sarah sank to the floor. "What am I gonna do with you?" He ran to her, her panties still in his mouth, and nudged her hand, begging for a pet.

Burying her face in his soft, fragrant fur, Sarah

hugged him and moaned before she glanced around her studio. One of her newest black pumps had the heel chewed off, her dirty clothes were strewn all over the floor and the newly-painted chair she had rescued from the dumpster last week now had bite marks on all four legs. As for the makeshift gate—a mounted but frameless movie poster of Sylvester Stallone as Rocky—that was supposed to contain her pup in the kitchen, it lay face down, all four corners chewed.

There was no way Sarah could keep this dog no matter how much she liked, no, loved him. She couldn't afford it.

Grant looked at his watch for the fifth time—2:55. Sarah had told him she'd be there at 2:30. He wondered whether she'd come in at all. Maybe it would be better if she didn't after his reaction to her in the bathroom last night, but he knew she wouldn't back out of her promise.

He strolled to the front to talk with his aunt who helped out as his receptionist until he could hire one fulltime. Right now, Grant could barely scrape together the rent, the loan payments and the daily supplies. Still, he loved being a vet, and had finally managed to make his dream of starting a clinic in Greer a reality last spring.

"She's not here yet, if that's what you want to know, and she hasn't called." The plump, dark-haired woman sat back in her chair and stared at him from over her bifocals, a grim expression crossing her features. "When are you going to learn that you can't save the world?"

Grant leaned against the counter and crossed his arms. "And when are you going to quit asking, Aunt Mary?"

Grant saw her look soften as she pulled her glasses from her nose. "Oh, you're just like your Uncle Gus. Always trying to help someone whether they want it or not."

She tapped at his elbow with her glasses. "Now straighten up, my sister taught you better manners than that. Here comes your new assistant."

Grant straightened and looked out the large windows as his aunt answered the ringing phone. Sarah was in the parking lot, bending over her bike. She'd come after all. A strange emotion shot through him and he swore it was relief. Late was better than never.

His heart lurched when he saw her face, set and determined, and the black bundle in the bike basket. She'd brought Rocky back. Something must have happened to make her change her mind.

He held his breath as she lifted the puppy from the basket, but expelled it quickly when he realized she was using the leash and collar he'd left at her apartment. He hoped he'd jumped to the wrong conclusion as he strode forward and opened the door.

"Hi Sarah. Hi Rocky." The furry bundle jumped on him, begging for attention. Scratching Rocky behind the ears, he sensed Sarah's agitation. Something was definitely wrong.

"Hi. Sorry I'm late. I . . ." Sarah looked at the floor, unable to make eye contact with him. "I had to work late, and had to deal with a few things when I got home and—"

"Did Rocky misbehave?"

She dredged up a half-smile. "I wouldn't have used that word exactly. Total destruction's more like it. I've a half-eaten shoe, a book report that has to be rewritten by tomorrow, and big brown stains on my carpet. I— I'm sorry, I can't keep him."

Sadness spread through her as she handed the leash to Grant. Overnight, she'd come to love the fluffball, but neither her landlord, nor her wallet could take the strain.

Still avoiding Grant's gaze, she looked at the poster of the happy family on the wall. Rocky belonged in a scene like that. Maybe someday, after she finished school, found a decent job and settled down, she could marry and have a child or two. Then she could have a dog like Rocky.

She swallowed the fierce emotions rising in her throat. Marriage? Children? Where had those ideas come from? She'd never thought about that before, but then again, she'd never met anyone like Grant.

When she was a child, she'd dreamed about acceptance, love and happiness—she'd longed to be part of a normal family—but those hopes died the day the

State stepped in and the harsh realities of life intruded. She'd learned that to protect herself, she had to shut her emotions down.

Like now. Sarah cleared her mind. A relationship with Grant wasn't possible. Relationships involved two people. She knew that from reading Lorraine's latest copy of *Cosmopolitan*. In fact, she'd failed the quiz miserably.

She wanted Grant—she couldn't deny the attraction she felt last night, even though the idea terrified her. Depending on someone else only led to disappointment and hurt. Things she'd had too much of in her life already.

"I'm sorry too." Grant spoke so softly, Sarah barely heard him over the low hum of the air conditioning unit. The tone of his voice matched her own glum mood and reminded her of her commitment. Her pride wouldn't allow her to walk away completely. She still had her debt to pay. "I'll work here as I promised until the bill is paid, Dr. Morrison."

Deep down, Sarah cried as Grant took hold of the leash. Years of practice held back the tears, but decades of longing rose to the surface. Sarah hid behind a mask of indifference. Most of the time it worked, but today, the thought of giving Rocky up nearly did her in.

She had no choice; her finances were too tight. School and rent ate up most of her money and what little was left barely put food on the table. She could make it alone, but she couldn't keep replacing what Rocky ruined. Sarah didn't dare think what she would do if she got kicked out of her apartment. She refused to go on government assistance. That was not in her plans for her new life.

Something must have shown in her face. "I have an idea." Grant handed Rocky back. "Don't give him up yet. Why don't you drop him off here before work, check on the boarded animals, and then take him home when you're done? That way, he won't be able to destroy anything else. You'll both be happier, and together."

The suggestion seemed almost too good to be true. Could she do that? Or would that put her even more in debt to the doctor? Sarah sighed, sank to her knees and rubbed the tufts of hair behind Rocky's ears. He grunted in contentment and stretched his neck out for more.

Sarah crumbled. Rocky touched her deep inside. She'd been nuts to think she could give him up so easily. Still, she wasn't completely convinced Grant's suggestion could work. She looked up at the man standing next to her. Her defenses wavered. "At five in the morning?"

"Whatever time is convenient." Grant knelt too and began to massage the dog's back. As his hand connected with hers, Sarah's breath caught in her throat, yet she didn't remove her hand. His touch felt right, protective, strong enough to help her face the world.

For as long as she could remember, she'd fended for herself, depended on no one, asked for nothing. Yet in a heartbeat, or the touch of a hand, she wanted that to change.

Except wanting got her only heartache.

"I could use your help, Sarah." Grant squeezed her hand lightly. "And remember, the extra time would get your bill paid off sooner."

Disappointment coursed through her. She should've known better. He didn't harbor any thoughts for her other than that of an employee no matter what silly ideas danced through her head. He wanted her to make his life easier. Not quite the same as a government check, but close enough in her book. Some things never changed.

"I don't know." Despite her weakening, Sarah couldn't give in completely. "I have night school three times a week. I'd still have to worry about Rocky then." She tried to pull her hand out from under his but his grip was firm.

She could have sworn she heard him sigh.

"Look. It's up to you. I'm trying to give you another option here. I'll give you a key so you can leave him here and take him home when you're done. You can also borrow a kennel until he's housebroken. As for the chewing, I'd suggest a couple of toys, but you don't have to pay the bill if you don't want to keep him."

Sarah looked into Grant's dark-blue eyes. They

were so deep she could swim in them. She shifted uncomfortably, instantly transported back to home number four.

Her foster sister stood next to her at the edge of the lake, a taunting sneer on her lips. "Go on, Sarah. It's not deep. You're not scared are you?"

So Sarah went in, knowing the lake was off-limits without adult supervision. How was she to know the bottom dropped suddenly into the inky stillness way over her head? At least there, she knew how to swim. Here she floundered, unable to look away, feeling herself sink into the unknown depths without a life vest and her hands tied behind her.

"I do want to keep him." Sarah swallowed, struggling to regain her composure. If everything worked out, as Grant believed it would, she'd be able to keep Rocky. But she'd also be indebted to him forever. No amount of time at the clinic could repay him for his generosity and the fact that for some crazy reason he trusted her. It was a risk she had to take. "If you're sure it's no problem, I'll accept your offer, and the kennel. But why are you doing this?"

"Doing what?"

"Being so—so kind," she whispered, barely able to form the words caught in her throat.

Grant stared at the woman beside him. For a second, her pale, heart-shaped face radiated longing, mingled with bewilderment, before a wall descended, shutting him out. Disappointment tugged at his heart but he wasn't surprised by her actions. It only added more fuel to that damned protective streak he harbored for strays.

He stood and held out his hand to help her rise. "I treat all my employees this way." He was lying. He didn't really treat his employees the way he wanted to treat Sarah. He only had two and they were both family; his Aunt Mary whom he had known all his life and his 17-year-old niece, Amanda, his sister Patty's daughter, who came in every few days to help out.

No. He sure didn't want to consider Sarah one of the family. Right now he wanted to hold her in his arms and kiss away the doubts, the sadness, the hesitation he saw in her eyes. But he couldn't. She was his employee.

Still, she brought out an instinct in him he couldn't ignore. Regardless of what Gillian said, he couldn't turn his back on someone in need, even though he knew Sarah would never ask.

Grant straightened his shoulders again. "Come into my office a second, Sarah, and bring Rocky so he stays out of trouble." He gave her a reassuring smile before motioning her to follow him. "You'll need something to wear while you're here. Have a seat." As he waved her into a brown leather chair that matched his, Grant pulled another sack from beneath his mahogany desk and handed it to her, hoping she liked it, and would accept it as a gift.

He watched in apprehension as she reached in the

bag and pulled out the colorful smock with cartoon characters of dogs printed all over. With some hesitation, she put it on. It fit her small frame perfectly. "For me? To keep?"

"Yes. It's a gift, unless you want to add it to your tab." Grant tried to keep the uncertainty from his voice as he leaned back in his chair. "I'd rather you didn't."

"Thank you, Dr. Morrison." She paused a second as if making a decision. "I'll accept your gift. So, what are my duties here, I've wasted enough of your time today."

Grant was amazed at how she could school her emotions so quickly. At the sight of the lab coat, her face shone with emotion, but in the next second that wall descended again. What had happened to Sarah that a simple gesture—a gift—could produce such a reaction? What caused her wariness, her reluctance, that chip on her shoulder?

"It's not a waste of time giving my staff a proper uniform," Grant said as he lifted himself from his chair, "but the afternoon is slipping away. Come on."

He accompanied Sarah out of the office and pointed to the hallway to his left that led to the back. She turned and started walking. Grant followed. The coat looked perfect on her, just like he knew it would. Too perfect. It did nothing to cover her curves. He should have gotten the pullover kind. It would have been less distracting.

The rest of the afternoon sped by as he detailed her

duties, explained the equipment, and showed her where to find everything. It pleased him that she caught on quickly. Especially when it came to dealing with Mrs. Wang and her overweight dog, Pugsley, who had tangled with the neighbor's cat again. Sarah's soothing touch calmed the dog while he cleaned and dressed the wounds.

As Grant hustled them out the front door, he left Sarah to sweep the back room. The sound of her humming a song he'd never heard followed him as he closed for the evening. It amazed him how she'd livened up the place in the few short hours she'd been here.

He looked at his watch. Aunt Mary had left a while ago, minutes after his overwrought client scurried through the door. It would be after 6 before he left. Too late to pick up something to cook for dinner and too soon to impose himself on his sister for another home-cooked meal. Grant's stomach growled as he began turning off the lights.

From the back room, he heard Sarah saying goodnight to the two dogs and a cat staying overnight before she and Rocky walked to the foyer.

"Is that everything, doctor? I need to go if I want to make it home before dark. The light is out on my bike."

Bathed in the fiery glow of sunset, she looked small and frail. He didn't like the idea of her riding the streets of Greer at dusk. "Call me Grant, remember?

Why don't I give you a ride? If you're going to take the kennel home you'll need help."

A frown creased her brow as she looked from Rocky to the medium-sized kennel Grant had placed by the reception desk. "I don't suppose there's any way it can be tied onto the back of my bike, is there?"

Grant raked a hand through his hair. "I'm sure there is, but by the time we figure it out, it'll be dark."

Indecision tugged at the corners of her mouth. "True. Whatcha think, Rocky? Want to ride in the doctor's car?"

Grant saw her whole demeanor change to what he interpreted as joy as the black dog wiggled his body and licked the back of her hand.

"That settles that," Sarah answered evenly. "Can it all fit?"

"Of course, or I wouldn't have offered." Grant played with his bottom lip. Maybe he could use this moment to draw Sarah out once they were outside the office. He wanted to know what went on inside that flaming red head of hers. "There is one catch though. I want you to join me for pizza tonight."

Chapter Four

"Pizza?" Sarah's hand gripped Rocky's leash tighter. She couldn't really afford to go out for pizza, and she would not let Dr. Morrison, no, Grant pay for her share.

"Why not? I'm hungry and I know you must be too."

Her stomach grumbled at the thought of a loaded pie with extra cheese. How long had it been since she'd had the luxury? "But—"

"I'm sure your day has been hectic." He cut her off as he glanced at Rocky and grinned. "No. I know your day has been hectic. Come here, boy."

Rocky bounded toward Grant. Caught off guard, the dog dragged Sarah with him. She released the leash just as Rocky jumped up against Grant's leg, or she might have joined him in Grant's arms.

She wasn't sure being held by Grant would be a bad thing, if he'd do it. No one, not even Mrs. White from her childhood, the only person who'd given a hoot about her before she became a ward of the state, had little time for affection. Sarah had known her old neighbor a lot longer.

It didn't matter that the look Grant was giving her reminded her of her building's resident tomcat, who had just cornered his prey, waiting to take one delectable nibble after another. Looks and actions were deceiving.

She should know. Too many times the people around her, who were supposed to love and care for her, turned their backs when she became an inconvenience. No one would get close enough to hurt her again. She'd make sure of that. Not even the man with the incredibly sexy blue eyes and Cheshire cat grin.

"I can't. I've got to retype the report Rocky ate this morning. Besides, what would we do with him? I doubt the restaurant would let us bring a dog inside."

His hands stilled on Rocky's head. "Down, boy." The searching look he gave her sent a shiver down her spine. "I can't do anything about your report, but we could leave Rocky here, or kennel him in my van, or take him to your place. I'd like you to come tonight, but it's up to you."

The empty feeling in her stomach remained, reminding her she hadn't eaten since those two pieces of raisin toast this morning, and she didn't have a thing ready for dinner. By the time she pieced a meal together, it would be late.

Sarah changed her mind. She had to eat to keep her energy up to redo her report. The extra money she earned today in Mabel's absence would more than cover her share.

"Okay. I'll go eat with you as long as I pay for my share. As for Rocky," she clapped her hands, taking the dog's attention away from the bags of dog food piled in the corner, "he'll have to get used to his kennel now, but I need to get some more food for him. I'm sure pizza isn't in his diet."

"It isn't. Let's get you another starter bag." A look of relief mixed with anticipation flashed across his features before Grant grabbed a small bag of food from the shelf, and placed it inside the kennel she'd reluctantly asked to borrow when she'd found out the cost of a new one. "Let me show you how to close so we can leave."

Sarah followed him watching every move.

"Of course," Grant continued, "I don't expect you to remember everything at once. Your main concern is walking the kenneled dogs and making sure all the animals have fresh food and water. I'll take care of the answering system and the front lights when I come in."

"You won't be here?"

"At five? I don't think so. I don't wake up until six." Grant smiled at her before he walked toward the back exit, turning off more lights as he went. "You can manage, but I'll leave you my phone number, just in case."

"Why do you trust me?" The words were out before she could stop them. Once voiced, they clung to the air, suffocating all other thoughts. Sarah could have kicked herself. That was why she'd moved to a small town. One where no one knew her past, or her troubles.

Silence fell on the narrow hallway as he turned to face her, concern knitted his brow. "Is there a reason why I shouldn't?"

Sarah hesitated. If Grant ever found out about parts of her past—incidents she wasn't too proud of, but had to do in order to survive on the streets—he'd send her away. She hadn't come this far to ruin the life she was making for herself.

Since her last brush with the law seven years ago, Sarah had managed to find steady work, buy a junk car, and keep a roof over her head. Now she was back in school to further her education. Nothing would make her go back to the life she'd put behind her. Nothing. Forcing those thoughts from her head, she crossed her fingers. What Grant didn't know wouldn't hurt him. "No."

She lied in more ways than one. Right now, she couldn't even trust herself not to throw herself at him.

She clenched her hands to keep from reaching out and feeling his warmth push away the coldness in her life.

Grant pushed it away for her.

"Sarah?" He cupped her chin in his hand and caressed it gently. Flames ignited where his touch left its mark on her skin. She struggled for air as the heat consumed her, but couldn't step away.

For too long, she'd felt nothing.

"If I had any doubts, I wouldn't be giving you the keys, would I?" he said, leaning closer to her. His gaze penetrated hers as if trying to read into the depths of her soul. Sarah shuddered involuntarily and closed her eyes to block out his image and rebuild her defenses.

She still couldn't reach out to him. She'd reached out before—to her parents, her numerous foster parents, her counselors—only to be pushed away. Rejected.

Never again. Maybe he was different from the others. Maybe not. She didn't want to know.

Whining, Rocky jumped up and nudged at her hand. Easing her fist, she massaged the warm fur on his head. The action brought some comfort. So did the fact that Rocky had stepped between them, forcing Grant to take a small step backward. Sadness coursed through her, though the space gave her room to breathe.

"Come on, I'm starved."

His words came out a husky whisper, slipping around her shoulders like a well-worn overcoat. One she could get used to but wouldn't. Her stomach rumbled in agreement as he led her to the back door.

"Here's where it gets tricky." Grant stopped in front of a security alarm panel and waited. "The code is six-four-one. An alarm will sound when you open the door." He handed her a set of keys from the front of his jean pocket. "A beep will sound until you punch in the code. Do you think you can do it?"

As she recovered from the unfamiliar emotions Grant evoked, Sarah frowned. Of course she could. She was very familiar with alarms. Intimate in fact. She didn't dare tell him she could probably disable the thing in less time then she could punch in his code thanks to her juvenile delinquent foster brother, Jim, in home number five.

As preteens, she and Jim had often escaped out of the house in Oakland to carouse the town without their foster parents' knowledge. She also knew how to hotwire a car, though she drew the line at theft. Something Jim had never learned. The last she heard, he was in jail.

"Sarah?"

She punched in the numbers. "I suppose we have thirty seconds to get out, don't we?" She opened the door and stepped outside, Rocky at her side.

Grant picked up the kennel and followed behind her. "You learn quick." He pulled the door shut, then used his own keys to lock it. As he turned, a smile lit his lips when he saw the comical scene developing in front of him.

When Rocky had sensed a bit of freedom, he took off running to the nearest bush. Taken by surprise by the sudden jerk, leash in hand, Sarah stumbled behind him. "Rocky, you bad boy. Where are your manners!"

Rocky led her from tree to bush to the fire hydrant, marking his territory. Grant had to talk to her again about having Rocky neutered. He knew Sarah wouldn't let him do the surgery free, so he'd add it to her bill.

A bill Grant had traded out for her services to keep her close to him. He didn't have time to mull over that revelation. The pup had caught sight of the stray cat Grant had been feeding in hopes of capturing her for spaying, and took off again with Sarah at his heels. Grant dropped the kennel and ran to help as the feline clawed her way up the tree and clung to an overhanging branch.

"Rocky, stop, you beast. Leave the poor kitty alone." She struggled to contain him. Rocky reared up, his paws digging at the air, and started barking at the calico mix who stared back, unblinking.

Grant stopped and chuckled at the sight when he realized Rocky wasn't going to drag Sarah across the main street. His laughter died as Sarah turned to look at him. He'd remembered too late she didn't appreciate his sense of humor and he'd blown it again because of his carelessness. To his utter amazement, she joined him, her laughter washing over him, chasing away his uneasy feeling.

With the onset of nightfall, Grant could feel the slight hint of fall in the air as he approached Sarah and the barking dog. "Can I make a suggestion?"

"What? Rocky, be quiet." She tugged on the leash, but the dog kept straining for the cat, his bark echoing off the brick building. Sarah was losing the battle.

He reached over and took the leash from her hands. "No!" He spoke sternly and pulled back, quieting the dog instantly. "Good boy." Squatting, he began to scratch the dog behind his ears, then under his chin, before he cocked his head to look at Sarah. "The local pet shop offers obedience classes. You might want to sign up for some training before Rocky gets any bigger."

"Bigger?" He saw her eyebrows raise at the question. "Bigger? And how big is this beast going to get?"

Grant wished he'd kept his mouth shut, but he knew it would be best for Sarah, Rocky, and all the cats in the neighborhood if the dog learned obedience. He continued to pet Rocky, unsure if he should answer the question.

"How *big* is he going to get? What kind of dog is he anyway?"

"I'd say he's definitely a black lab mix and . . ." Grant hesitated for a split second.

"And what?" Her eyes shone like fire in the light thrown off by the street lamp. Her hair had taken on a life of its own as her bun loosened, creating a halo around her face. Part angel, part devil. He just didn't know which side would emerge when he told her the truth.

"Part rottweiler and maybe some chow. He's probably going to weigh at least ninety pounds."

"Ninety pounds? Why, that's almost as much as I weigh." Sarah groaned and put a hand to her head. "Only I could run over a dog that, when he's grown, is going to be bigger than me. How am I going to fit him in my basket?"

"You're not." Grant stood and dusted his pants.

Another silence stretched between them in the still evening. Only the sound of a car turning the corner, it's tires crunching against some loose stones interrupted them.

"You knew this afternoon when you made me the offer I couldn't refuse in order to keep him, didn't you?" She knelt and hugged Rocky. Grant watched her struggle for calm as Rocky broke free and began licking her face. "You knew I'd fall in love with him and not be able to give him up no matter how big, or how much trouble he got into."

"To be honest? Yes, Sarah, I'd hoped so. You and Rocky seem right for each other, but my original offer still stands. If you don't want to keep him, I'll try and find someone else to take him in." *Probably myself.* He'd taken a liking to the pup, not to mention the owner. Grant knew he was playing with fire.

"You're something else. Has anyone ever told you that?" Sarah laughed at the situation. This afternoon she was ready to give her friend up, and now she was planning on taking him to an obedience class. Except she wasn't the proud owner of a dog, but of a horse. Mr. Baxter was definitely going to have a fit—and so was her wallet.

Her stomach whined in protest again. Wallet or not, pizza sounded good with or without Grant. She preferred the former, although she knew it was not in her best interests for self-preservation. "Let's go. I'm going to need lots of strength to handle him."

She unlocked her bike and walked toward the only vehicle in the back parking lot. "A van? You don't look like a van person."

Grant shrugged. "I make housecalls to some of my elderly patients."

This man was too good, too kind. There had to be a catch. There always was. Sarah looked inside after he disarmed the security locks and pulled back the side door. The back seats had been taken out leaving plenty of room to stow her bike and Rocky's temporary kennel among several other kennels lined up against the back wall.

He must have noticed that she studied them. "I also work with the town picking up strays."

Grant never ceased to amaze her. The more she learned about this man, the more she liked him, and the more she scared herself for liking him.

A companionable silence accompanied them as Grant drove to another section of town Sarah had never seen. He parked in front of a tiny pizza parlor, just off the tree-lined street. The name, Tony's Pizza, written in red neon letters in the bay window, showed brazenly in the night.

"Be a good boy, Rocky, and I'll give you extra treats later." At the sound of his sad grunt, she blew her dog a kiss and exited the vehicle before she changed her mind.

"It doesn't look like much, but it's the best pizza in Greer." His grasp on her arm seemed to take on an intimate, almost possessive feel as he led her inside the quaint, brick building with the green awnings. Her heart skipped a beat as she leaned into him, absorbing his strength. For a second, no more. She didn't need anyone to ease her pain. But it felt nice, just the same.

The delicious smell of tangy tomatoes and melted cheese wafted into her nostrils, while the sounds of clanging silverware and the low buzz of conversation greeted her ears. Sarah's mouth watered as the hostess, whom Grant had called Christine, sat them in a corner booth.

A burning candle held by a well-used Chianti bottle covered in wax graced the center of a red-and-white checked tablecloth. Pictures of Italy covered the walls. Silk plants and knick-knacks lined wooden shelves suspended from the relief tin ceilings, and numerous fans kept the air circulating. Sarah liked the place immediately.

"Hey, Grant." A perky blonde in her early 20s, dressed in jeans, a gingham shirt and a tiny black apron, appeared. "Long time no see." She winked. "The usual?"

Sarah's heart fluttered at the girl's flirtation. She studied the menu, wondering if Grant had a girlfriend or worse, a wife. She hadn't seen a ring, but she'd seen the numerous pictures on his desk this afternoon when he'd given her the coat. She was sure several were of his family, but the portrait of a smiling brunette made her a little edgy. She'd been accused of lots of things, but having dinner with a married man wasn't one of them. He didn't act like one, but Sarah had little experience with men in general.

"Hi, Veronica. You bet. I hope Sarah can handle it."

At the mention of her name, Sarah's attention returned to the conversation between Grant and the waitress.

Veronica laughed. "Oh I'm sure she can if she can handle Ted's cooking at the diner." The girl extended her hand in Sarah's direction. "Hi. You must be that new Sarah in town. I'm Veronica, Mabel's granddaughter. My grandma's told me about you working at the diner and all, said you were the best server they'd hired in a long time. She also said you couldn't miss the red hair. That's how I knew it was you. So how'd you hook up with Grant?"

Sarah sat speechless as her hand sought to cover the curly hair escaping her bun. Mabel was another busybody, almost as bad as her neighbor, Mrs. Maddox.

"Sarah's helping me at the clinic a few days a week." Grant threaded his fingers through hers. "Sorry. It's a small town. People don't have anything better to do than talk, do they Veronica?"

At the warmth of Grant's touch and the no-nonsense tone of his voice, a rush of pleasure swept through her.

"Nope. Welcome to Greer, Sarah. I hope you like our small, boring town." A bell rung from the kitchen and Veronica looked over her shoulder. "Got an order up, I'll be right back."

As the whirl of energy left, Sarah sank back into the wooden booth. She liked the girl. "She's nice."

Sarah saw Grant smile at the waitress' retreating back as he picked up the salt shaker and spun it between his palms. "Veronica's a live one, for sure. She's dating my younger brother, Matthew."

"Oh." Not knowing what else to say, Sarah stared at the words written inside the menu until Veronica returned and plunked down a pitcher of beer and two iced mugs on their table. With a wave, she was off again. "None for me." Sarah placed her hand over the top of her mug. She'd never touched a drop and never would. Not after she watched what alcohol had done to her parents when they were alive. She would not repeat their mistakes. "I don't drink, but don't let me stop you."

Grant poured himself some of the frothy brew and took a sip. "What brought you to Greer, Sarah? The town's not much more than a boring dudsville in central California?"

He watched her intently, which made her nervous. She should've known Grant would start asking questions. Questions she didn't want to answer because they brought back a past she was trying to forget. Though for a moment, she considered telling him. Sarah shuddered at the thought of what his reaction would be. She reached for her water glass and drained the contents. "It's really a dull story, not one you'd want to hear. What about you? You grew up here, didn't you?"

"You first. I'm sure anything that concerns you could hardly be dull."

Sarah knew he expected an answer. A truthful one at that. She sighed. Because of his kindness, she decided to give him a short one with just enough information to satisfy his curiosity, but not enough to reveal what she wanted to leave behind. Most people didn't understand.

She twisted a stray piece of hair around her finger. "I'm from the Bay area originally. Oakland. Then I went to Sacramento for a while. Things didn't work out so I got in my car and drove. Greer was as far as

I got before the engine blew. I couldn't afford to fix it, so I stayed, got a job at the diner, an apartment, and started classes at Denton Community College. End of story. How about you?"

Grant knew there was a lot more to Sarah's story. Her hesitations, her defenses, her mannerisms all spoke more to him than her words. He sensed a lonely, scared woman hidden beneath those defenses. He tried to put a tight reign on his budding emotions.

"You're right. I was born and raised here. Got into college on a scholarship, went to vet school, then came back and opened my practice to be close to my family."

He'd given her just as vague an answer. No need to mention his financial problems, or the fact that he was starting to care for Sarah, even though he hardly knew anything about her.

As he looked at the woman sitting across from him, a war raged inside him over his need to help her and his need to stay emotionally detached because she was his employee. He lost the last battle. Against his better judgement, he became determined to draw her out a little each day.

Fortunately, their meal arrived. One medium deep-dish pie loaded with onions, mushrooms, green peppers, olives, and sausage. His stomach growled in anticipation. Tony's pizza was the best. After the pizza was devoured, he was sorry to see the evening begin to end. And even more sorry, but not surprised, when

Sarah refused to let him pay the entire bill. Rocky, however, was ecstatic when they let him out of his kennel for the ride to Sarah's building.

Grant insisted on accompanying them inside. He knew Sarah couldn't handle Rocky and carry the kennel and her lab coat at the same time, but she'd never ask for help. Not to mention that his mother would have his hide if she found out he'd simply dropped her off and left.

As they stood by her door in the dimly-lit hallway, he could see Sarah hesitate as she reached for her key, as if struggling with some inner conflict. He saw her gaze wander to the coat thrown over her arm, and he wanted to smooth away the worry lines creasing her forehead and kiss away her sorrows. "What's wrong, Sarah?"

The sound of the key turning in the lock broke the quiet. Her voice wavered with emotion as she turned to face him. "Did you really mean I could keep the lab coat?"

Her question astonished him. "Yes. It's a gift."

"No strings attached?"

"No. It's yours free and clear." Grant put Rocky's kennel down and ran his hand through his hair, perplexed at her question. "Why?"

He heard Sarah draw in a ragged breath. "Thanks. I've never gotten a gift before without strings attached." She opened the door, waved Rocky inside, and then dragged in the kennel. "Goodnight, Grant. I'll see you Thursday."

Grant stared at the closed door, his shock turning to anger at Sarah's parents. Attaching strings to a gift? Who could do that to a child?

Chapter Five

Sarah lay in bed that night, long after her newly-typed report sat on top of the refrigerator where Rocky couldn't reach it. Beside her, he seemed content, nearly asleep. His eyelids twitched, and he snorted as if he were chasing that calico cat in a delicious dog dream.

A sigh escaped her lips. If only she could do the same. But every time she closed her eyes, the image of Grant stood before her. Only she saw him standing with his arms open wide, beckoning, begging her to push aside her fears and let him comfort her. If only it were that easy.

Years of restraint and determination to hide her longing for acceptance were being peeled back by the generosity of one man. Grant Morrison. But it wouldn't last. It never did.

What a fool she'd been tonight at Tony's. For a split second, she'd considered telling him about her checkered past. Thank goodness her sanity stepped in and brought her back to reality.

She'd even been able to maintain that reality until she reached home. For one brief moment though, she'd forgot and let down her guard and had admitted something about her past. A mistake she wouldn't let happen again, even if she was attracted to him.

"No!"

A startled Rocky sat up and opened his eyes as she flopped onto her side and stared out the window where a large oak tree dominated her view. She could make out the leaves, which at 3 o'clock in the morning had taken on an almost ethereal quality in the silver moonlight.

Sarah closed her eyes from the beauty. What was she to do? Grant didn't seem to be like the rest of them, but her distrust of people, no matter how kind, would not allow her to think differently.

"Oh, Rocky." Sarah rolled back and gathered the dog closer. "What would I do without you." The puppy's warmth permeated her nightgown, chasing away the chill, as he nuzzled her arm with his nose. Rocky understood her and loved her for what she was—a tough, streetwise kid from Oakland, who needed no one, depended on no one, wanted no one. They'd found each other. That was enough.

* * *

In a few weeks, Sarah's routine became established. Every morning she woke before dawn, stopped by the clinic to care for the boarded animals, then pedaled off to the diner. By mid-afternoon, she was back at the clinic to work, or pick up Rocky on her days off, then off to her apartment, obedience class, or school.

Rocky had also settled into his routine, and his accidents at night had dwindled to an occasional puddle, which would make Mr. Baxter extremely happy. And thanks to chew toys and rawhide bones, he hadn't chewed up any more reports, shoes or clothing.

Obedience classes were going well too. Rocky had learned to walk properly on the leash and sit at her command. They were still having a problem with "Stay," but she had gained enough confidence to know her beloved pet would master that soon.

They were becoming a family, just the two of them. Though Sarah wondered if he'd ever forgive her for having him fixed. The sorrowful look on his face when she'd arrived that afternoon after the surgery was almost too much, but she didn't need any more dogs.

Especially ones of Rocky's size. He'd almost doubled in size and Sarah no longer tried to squeeze him into her basket. With some added help from the dog trainer and an extended leash, Rocky ran alongside her. Life was good.

Grant looked at his watch. Sarah was due any minute. In the time she'd worked for him, he liked what he saw in his new assistant—and not just her physical attributes. His trust in her had grown, as well as his emotional attachment, even though he knew better.

Still, he'd come to rely on her silent strength and quiet determination. No matter what task he assigned her, she was always ready and willing to do it. A natural with animals, she interacted with them better than with his customers, though her performance there was exemplary too. No, he could find no fault with Sarah, except for her reluctance to accept his generosity.

Rocky padded over to him, sighed, and laid his head down on Grant's knee as he examined the x-ray of Mr. Carr's cat. Sarah's dog had become an institution around the clinic. The clients loved him. And surprisingly, he was no bother. He patted his head, unable to concentrate. "Come on boy, let's take you outside before Sarah gets here."

Slipping the negative back in the folder, Grant leashed Rocky and headed for the back door. "A few minutes of fresh air will clear my brain." He looked down at the dog as they left the clinic. "What do you think?"

Rocky cocked his head and looked at Grant with a quizzical expression before he caught scent of another dog. Immediately, the animal barked and lunged for the opposite side of the parking lot.

Grant regained his balance and laughed. Not only at himself for talking to Sarah's dog, but at Rocky, whose obedience training seemed to go by the wayside at any tantalizing smell that caught his attention. "Still having trouble with the 'Heel' command, I see. We're going to have to do something about that."

"Rocky!" Sarah came wheeling across the lot, pedaling furiously. "I'm here. Did you miss me?" Grant released the leash just in time to keep from being pulled against Sarah and her bike.

Rocky jumped up and licked her face as his tail wagged furiously, making his whole body shake. At the look of pure joy on her face, all barriers down, Grant felt a twist in his gut. Over time, he'd begun to draw her out; finding out she loved chocolate, hated cold weather, and tolerated comedies, though she still kept him in the dark about anything regarding her past, which disappointed him.

She clammed up when he brought up the subject of her past, though he noticed a look of longing on her face when she stared at the poster of a smiling family on the wall. An idea formulated in his brain. He should know better but he couldn't change who he was.

"Hi. How was your day?" he questioned evenly, not wanting her to recognize how happy he was to see her. Not that she would notice since Rocky had thrust himself into her arms and was in the process of licking her.

"Down, Rocky." She laughed and pushed the dog off so she could dismount. "My day was fine. Sorry I'm late. Mabel was sick again, so Veronica came in.

I really like her." She looked up at him with a smile. "How was yours?"

"Pretty calm . . . so far."

That changed the minute Sarah brushed the dirt Rocky's paws had left on her powder-blue sweater. The color suited her, as did the lightweight material, which clung to her curves more than Grant wanted to think about.

For a moment, Grant stared at his assistant, lost in the mystery of her green eyes. The secrets that lay hidden behind their translucent color drove him mad, but there was nothing he could do for now. He'd seen her shut down too many times, erect too many walls the moment he pried too deep. But with any luck, that would change.

Her hair was pulled back into a bun as usual, but a few wisps had escaped, enhancing the softness of her face. Grant noticed several freckles graced the bridge of her upturned nose. They were appealing, like tempting pieces of candy, and seemed to beckon him to plant a tender kiss on each one. He took a step closer, then caught himself as he started to lean in. He cleared his throat and fought desperately for something to say.

"Speaking of Veronica, how about going out for pizza tonight?" There hadn't been time lately and he missed his usual pie, but he knew it wouldn't be the same without Sarah.

"Oh, thanks. I already have plans. Rocky is . . ." She

held a hand to her mouth and whispered, "He's getting a B-A-T-H. Aren't you, boy?"

"A B-A-T-H?" Grant mimicked her. Memories flashed back to the other time Sarah tried washing him. There was nothing sexy about giving a dog a bath unless you included a curvaceous redhead, a tiny bathroom and one wet, clingy purple T-shirt. "Need any help?"

"Thanks, but I think I can do it this time." Sarah answered coolly. Blood rushed to her cheeks as she turned away. Leave it to Grant to remember that embarrassing incident.

She headed into the clinic before taking Rocky off his leash. Even with his training, she didn't quite trust her dog not to sniff out that stray calico or any other animal.

"I'm sure you can." A disappointed Grant followed her. "It's been quiet today, there's not a lot to do. Why don't you take Rocky to the park or give him his B-A-T-H now?"

Sarah stopped in her tracks as the color fled from her face. Her bill couldn't be paid off. Sarah had figured on at least another month at the rate she was going with all the added expenses. The neutering, the chew toys, even the new bowl and leash cost money. Money Sarah didn't have but was more than willing to work for. Grant had offered to pay for them all, but she refused to accept his charity. She couldn't.

"Hey." He moved around in front of her and gently

lifted her chin, forcing her to gaze into his eyes. She didn't flinch "Just because there's nothing to do doesn't mean your job is done. I thought you'd like some time off. Play time. I don't think you get enough, that's all."

Sarah had never seen such tenderness, such compassion directed at her. And for the first time in a long time, believed it was all true. Mesmerized, she watched him lean closer and plant a light kiss on her lips.

It was all she could do not to reach out and wrap her arms around his neck, and explore unknown territory. In that instant, Sarah was glad to leave. She had to get out before she did something stupid, like kiss him back.

"Hi, Sarah. Mind if I come in?"

Taken back by his unexpected visit, she paused, then shook her head and held the door wider to admit a somewhat hesitant Grant. This time she knew his visit was more than just to check up on Rocky. Still reeling from this afternoon's crazy emotions, her voice wavered as she clutched her hands together. "Hi. A pizza from Tony's?"

"Yep. Sort of a peace offering. Since I couldn't entice you to go out for one, I brought it to you. I hope it doesn't upset your plans." Grant walked past her, juggling a pizza box in one hand and a bottle of soda in the other as the aroma of melted cheese, sauce and spices wafted by her nose. She remembered the smell well. Her mouth watered. The box of macaroni and cheese on the counter could wait.

"Not at all." Another lie slid past her lips. Her plan had been to spend the evening rebuilding the walls around her heart, not spend dinner with the man who intended to break them down. She might not have the education he had, but she had the street smarts and knew what he was trying to do. For the most part, it had been working. He'd gotten her to admit far more than she'd ever admitted before—even to her counselors.

Rocky's bark echoed through the apartment. "Here. Let me take that before Rocky makes you drop it." She gave him a slight smile as she lifted the box from his palm and held it securely between her hands just as her dog jumped over the makeshift gate and charged at Grant.

"Heel." The command didn't do any good since Sarah didn't have his choke collar on, but Grant didn't seem to mind. He knelt and petted her dog vigorously behind the ears until Rocky dropped onto his back. "I put him in the kitchen after his bath to dry, but I see it didn't work."

"Aha. I thought you smelled like a rose." His gaze on the dog, he rubbed Rocky's belly. The dog's paws scratched at thin air with pleasure. "And I can see you're hardly worse for the wear. Or you either."

At Grant's look, the intense longing returned. Who

was Sarah kidding? His mere presence affected her. It was all she could do to answer him. "The bath wasn't easy, but it wasn't a failure like the first time. I'm only a little wet. It's just going to take time. And Rocky's forgiven me, haven't you?" Her dog jumped up and nudged her hand. "Oh, you. You just want a piece of pizza."

She set the box down on her makeshift coffee table, which was a piece of plywood balanced on two milk crates, covered with a floral tablecloth. "Stay out, Rocky."

Grant's gaze met hers as she looked at him across the table. At his grin, her pulse quickened and her knees turned to jelly. She'd fallen for him, no question about it. Forget about her earlier plan. Her heart would never be completely safe again.

Suddenly, she felt . . . inadequate, dressed in damp purple sweats compared to his crisp Oxford shirt and khaki pants. "Um. I need to change. I'll be right back." She bolted from the tiny room, grabbing a pair of jeans and a red sweater from the closet on her way to the bathroom.

Satisfied with her outfit, she glanced in the small mirror above the sink. Sarah gave her hair one last pat, opting to leave it down. She rarely went for the wild look, but tonight, something felt different, something felt right, regardless of how she felt earlier. It was as if she wanted Grant to see her in a different light. Not as an assistant, or a waitress, or even a charity case, but as a woman. She'd taken chances before, and most of them had turned out okay. Still, the idea scared the heck out of her as she applied a quick splash of cologne.

She exited the bathroom before she lost her nerve and walked over to flip on the radio, her only source of entertainment. Soft strains of a classic rock song chased away the silence. Since the sun had set, her apartment basked in an intimate glow, but with the light fading, Sarah switched on the overhead light to dispel the lengthening shadows. "Yum. Smells good."

Grant raised the lid of the box. "Let's eat."

"Hang on. Let me get some plates and napkins." Eating out of a box reminded her of when she lived on the streets. Those days were over, but the memories still haunted her.

"Let me help." Grant trailed her into the little alcove of a kitchen, no bigger than a closet with a stove, refrigerator and a few cabinets. "Where are your glasses?"

"In the cabinet left of the stove. Drat." Sarah bent over to pick up the fork she'd dropped on the floor. Grant watched mesmerized as the jean material stretched tight across her bottom.

"Is something wrong?" Sarah looked at him quizzically.

"No. Nothing." He retreated to the main room with two glasses in hand. How could he explain that he wanted to undress her, and that he didn't want it to stop there. Fortunately, Sarah couldn't read his mind as she settled herself on the floor across from him.

"Soda?"

"Yes, please," she answered, watching him as he unscrewed the lid of the liter of cola and poured it into two juice glasses. "Sorry I don't have the right glasses, I don't spend much time here."

"Don't apologize, any glass will do." He gave her a grin and lifted his glass. "Cheers. Let's eat before the pizza gets cold."

They devoured the pizza. Sarah occasionally gave a piece of crust to Rocky, who sat impatiently between them.

"That's not good for him."

"I know, but he's such a good boy." She leaned over and kissed Rocky on his nose. "Aren't you my sweet?" She fed him another bit of crust and he licked her face. "Do you have any dogs? You never mentioned it."

"Yes. Two."

"Two? Why don't you bring them to the clinic?"

"Max and Matilda are Queensland Heelers, and very territorial. It's easier to leave them at home." At this moment, Grant himself was feeling territorial also.

The carefree look Sarah gave him sent his body into overdrive. Something had changed since he'd arrived. Her apprehension had disappeared along with the pizza. With her hair down, the soft curls falling carelessly around her shoulders made Sarah look every inch available. He wondered if she had any idea the affect she had on him.

"Max and Matilda? Those are interesting names. Can you honesty tell me you don't feed them table scraps? How can you look at their precious little faces and not share what you have?" Rocky licked her face again.

This stray dog had done wonders for her, softening her around the edges and breaking down some of her barriers. He was glad he'd convinced her to take Rocky home. Insanely enough, he wanted her to let him in her life too.

"You're right." He gave Rocky the last bit of crust on his plate. "I have a soft heart for my dogs, but I try to keep their scraps healthy. Promise me you won't feed him pork or chicken bones. They can splinter in his throat. And don't feed him chocolate. It can be toxic."

"Don't worry. I won't."

As Sarah cleaned up the mess, he looked around the apartment. The last time he was here, he hadn't had the chance to notice his surroundings. Bare beige walls met a white ceiling and tan carpet, which had brown splotches on it because of Rocky. He had to remember to get her a bottle of spot remover so her landlord wouldn't get mad.

Other than the spots, the room had an almost sterile look to it. The only furniture in the room was the daybed where he sat, a blue dresser in the corner, a painted chair with all four legs chewed—courtesy of Rocky he was sure—and the table in front of him.

Odd, there were no pictures. No family, no friends, not one even of herself. Nothing personal about her at all. Perplexed, he thought of his own place. Pictures graced his walls and tables, all gifts from his mother and sisters, but still, he had something to identify with as family.

Sarah returned and sat down, as Grant refilled their glasses. He looked around her apartment again. "Why don't you have any pictures of your family?"

"I have no family."

A closed look on her face replaced the open one she'd worn earlier, but Grant decided not to let the moment pass. He was emotionally involved with Sarah whether he liked it or not and he wanted her to open up, accept his friendship, accept him. "None at all? I won't judge you, Sarah, if that's what you're afraid of. You can tell me."

"No. I can't."

Grant could hear the tightness in her voice and see the pain in her eyes. The way she seemed to shrink in upon herself as if wrestling with some inner demons stabbed him like daggers. He couldn't stand it any longer. Sarah needed him, needed his help whether she realized it or not.

"Yes, you can." He settled next to her and wrapped his arms around her. It felt so right to hold her against him as he rested his chin on her head. She didn't fight him off. Instead, with a shudder she melted into him.

The idea of telling Grant terrified her but she felt close to him tonight. Somehow, she knew she'd feel better to share some of her secrets. She hadn't realized it then, but baring part of her soul was the choice she'd made when she let her hair down in the bathroom. Her attraction for him had blossomed into love, which would only hurt her in the end, but for tonight, she didn't care.

A sigh escaped her lips as she leaned into him, accepting his strength, even if it was just for a moment. "Biologically, I once had parents, if the people that produced me in the back seat of a Chevy could be called that. But they didn't care about me. They didn't care if I was hungry, thirsty, or dirty. They'd lived from one alcoholic binge to the next. If it hadn't been for the neighbor in the trailer next door, I probably wouldn't have even learned to walk or talk. If anyone was family, it was my neighbor, Mrs. White."

"Oh, Sarah."

Grant held her, as if trying to absorb her pain, which was impossible. But after all these years, it felt good to tell another person. She had to continue. "Finally, when I was eight, my parents died in a drunk driving accident. I spent years in the foster circuit, bounced from one home to another until I was eighteen. I hit the road and never looked back. You know the rest."

That wasn't exactly true. What she didn't tell him would probably come back to haunt her.

Chapter Six

The next morning, Grant found a spring in his step that hadn't been there before. The day had dawned crisp and bright as he went for his morning jog now that he had the luxury of resuming since Sarah went to the clinic in the mornings to take care of the animals. Cool air filled his lungs, making him feel younger than his 30 years.

He waved to his neighbor retrieving the morning paper across the way. "Morning, Jack."

"Morning, Grant. Joyce mentioned something about bringing Sebastian in. Do you have time today?"

"I always have time for you. Tell her ten o'clock would be great. See you later."

Grant resumed his run, listening to the leaves crunch under his feet. Fall was his favorite season, and this year proved to be no different. Mother Nature had certainly outdone herself by providing a spectacular burst of yellows, reds and oranges on the old elm and oak trees lining the street. A light breeze blew, rustling the leaves overhead.

By next month, the remaining leaves would drop as the days grew shorter. The stark contrast of bare trees reaching their limbs to the gray-stained sky had always fascinated him. He wondered what season Sarah liked the most.

Sarah. Last night was a revelation. She'd given away another piece of her identity, allowing him to understand her better. Her walls were a defense mechanism, meant to protect her from what must have been a life from hell. Grant could only wonder at the things that happened, not wanting to give voice to the horrible things that crossed his mind.

He also realized the information she'd given him hadn't been easy, and he was glad he hadn't kissed her again like he'd done in the office. Because this time, he didn't think it would be a light peck on the lips. His body had ached for it, but he wasn't sure Sarah was ready for that kind of intimacy. With the few barriers down, Grant might be able to span the vast gulf that still lay between them. A few more weeks and maybe he would know the whole story. He sure wanted to.

He gulped in the fresh air as his feet pounded against the asphalt. Something about Sarah brought out his protective streak and touched him deep inside. Maybe it was her shyness and her vulnerability, or maybe it was, in spite of everything, he still believed in doing good things for others. He knew there were things he could do for Sarah. He could start by chasing away those unhappy memories and creating some sort of stability in her life.

Running by the old high school, Grant waved at the custodian before he looped around and headed home. Mr. Cruz had been there ever since his parents had attended Greer High. Rumor had it he was retiring after this year. Grant wondered who'd clean the spit-wads from the bathroom ceilings and extricate the laboratory frogs flushed down the toilets before they backed up the plumbing.

Not that *he* had ever been guilty of doing any of those pranks. Had Sarah ever done any stunts like that? There was still so much he didn't know about her. So much he wanted to find out, but if he wasn't careful, he might scare her back into the shell he'd finally managed to crack.

Invigorated from his run, Grant was surprised—and happy—to see two people waiting for him in the clinic when he arrived. The ad he'd started to run in the local paper must be working. Business had picked up the last few days.

Aunt Mary was doing her best to keep track of a conversation on the phone while the chocolate lab barked at the caramel-colored cat huddled in the corner of its kennel.

Grant wished Sarah was there to settle the fray.

"Hi. I'm Dr. Morrison." He greeted the stranger who had just finished filling out the necessary paperwork before turning his attention to his mother's friend.

"Hi, Mrs. Polk, trouble with Misty today?" He nodded toward the dog. "Come on back."

Grant glanced at the information the thin, graying woman had handed him. "Aunt Mary put Mrs. Williams and Taffy in room two. I'll be right in." He motioned Mrs. Polk to follow him.

The first half of the morning flew by. After his fourth patient, a cat with nothing more than a hairball, Grant lifted his arms over his head and stretched. Ten o'clock and he missed Sarah.

Her silent strength, her attention to details, her quiet calm was what he needed at his side. But while Sarah was more efficient, his aunt's skill at the books couldn't be beat.

If only he could have Sarah work for him fulltime, but Grant knew he couldn't pay her what she was worth. At least not yet. He'd only been open six months. The ad, the animal health articles he wrote, and word of mouth helped, but he was still a long way from justifying the added expense. His loan payment, plus the rent and supplies stretched the budget tight.

But he didn't regret opening the clinic when he did.

Aside from Dr. Witherspoon, who was ready to retire in a few years time, the only other clinics were 5 miles away in Denton. With the growing population, Greer needed his services. His increasing business attested to that.

The tone Grant installed in the back signaled the arrival of another client. That had to be Joyce Thompson with Sebastian. Reviewing their chart, Grant pulled out the needed vaccinations from the drawer and set them on the counter as he heard his aunt and neighbor walk down the hall.

"Hi, Grant."

"Hi, Joyce. Aunt Mary, I need you to find me that box of syringes we ordered." He took the kennel from his aunt's hand and lifted it on the examining table. The black cat didn't look too happy, but then again, a visit to the vet couldn't be high on the list of priorities that included eating, sleeping, and chasing the neighborhood birds. "Come here, fella." He opened the door and pulled Sebastian out.

As the feline huddled on the table, he looked into his round, green eyes and noticed they were the same color as Sarah's. Her image clouded his vision; her scent invaded his nostrils. A minute didn't seem to pass that he didn't think about his assistant.

Shaking his head, he folded the cat's ears back to check for mites, examined his teeth, then felt his body from head to tail. He placed the stethoscope in his ears and listened to his heartbeat. Everything sounded normal.

"Good boy." He scratched the cat under the chin and listened to him purr. Would Sarah do that if he scratched her there? The idea amused him. One of these days he'd have to find out.

"So what time does your new assistant come in, Grant? I've heard so much about her and wanted to meet her."

"Two-thirty." Aunt Mary spoke for him, returning with the needles. The edge in her voice surprised him. What was bothering her? He thought his aunt had gotten over her wariness of Sarah, but her attitude challenged his thinking.

Grant grabbed the syringes and placed them on the counter next to the vials.

"Oh dear. Needles. Where's the bathroom?"

Grant noticed the color had fled Joyce's face. "Down the back hall to your right. We'll be done in a few minutes." He didn't fill the first syringe with the feline leukemia shot until his neighbor was out of sight.

"Why don't you like Sarah?" He threw the empty vial away and administered the shot.

"It's not that I don't like her," his aunt started, "it's—I don't trust her, that's all. I haven't since the day she walked in the door. She's so quiet—so secretive." She handed him another vial. "Why Mrs. Walker down at the pharmacy says—"

"Mrs. Walker doesn't have a nice word to say about anyone." Grant grabbed another vial, extracted the vaccine and injected the unhappy cat.

"Well, it is true that Sarah just showed up in town one day, in a broken down car that Mr. Halverson at the auto shop said can't be fixed. Then she took a temporary job over at the Greer's Diner."

"If she's here temporarily, how do you explain her attending classes at Denton Community College?"

"I can't, but I've seen her type before and I'm worried about you. I know you think you can help her—"

Grant held up his hand to stop her, but she continued.

"What do you know about her? She's a drifter. Mark my words, she'll be here one day and gone the next. I don't want to see you hurt, that's all." With a shaking hand, his aunt settled her glasses on her nose before handing him the vial of rabies vaccination.

He extracted the liquid into the syringe. That's one thing Grant hated about living in a small community. Everyone knew everyone else's business.

As for Sarah, what did he really know about her? He knew she was orphaned at an early age and spent years in foster homes, but he wouldn't enlighten his aunt, and give her more feed for the rumor mill. He knew Sarah had moved around a lot, but had given no specific reasons. On a whim, would she leave again, taking his heart with her?

"I'm a grown boy, Aunt Mary. I can take care of

myself." Bunching the hairs at the base of the cat's neck, Grant injected the shot. Was he a fool for trusting Sarah? Could he really take care of himself? After last night, he wasn't so sure. He'd started to fall in love with his assistant.

"That's what I'm afraid of."

At the sigh of resignation, Grant glanced at his aunt. Worry lines creased her forehead as she chewed the pink lipstick off her bottom lip. He'd never seen her in such a state. Something was up and he knew he wasn't going to like it. "What aren't you telling me?"

"I asked Gillian's boyfriend, Joe, to run her plates."

"You what?"

Joyce returned, ending their conversation.

Grant should have been an actor. In a wink, his professional demeanor replaced his shock at his aunt's admission. "You're all set." He no sooner opened the door to the kennel and the cat leaped inside. Grant smiled in spite of himself and closed the gate. "And I thought you liked it here, Sebastian. Thanks for coming in today, Joyce. Aunt Mary will see you out."

Feeling the need for some fresh air, Grant hooked the leash to Rocky's collar and headed out the back door. Maybe a good walk would settle him down. While Aunt Mary had no right to request that information, he knew she was only looking out for him. Family was like that.

Even after a quick walk around the block, his mood hadn't lifted. Could his aunt see something he couldn't? Maybe he should do some checking up on his own, but that thought disturbed him.

He shook his head, trying to dispel the seeds of doubt planted in his brain. They were nonsense. Sarah was nothing like the picture certain people were painting. The trust he saw in her eyes behind the wall of defenses was real. She didn't lie or cheat, he'd bet his practice on it.

Sarah was only too glad to leave the noisy confines of the diner and step into the comforting interior of the clinic. She inhaled deeply, filling her lungs with the tangy scent of disinfectant, not the smell of stale grease.

A chorus of barks greeted her as she passed by the room to her right. "Hi, guys. What were you in for today?" Stopping in front of the kennels, she reached in and petted the smaller of the two brown dogs, then gave a hearty scratching to the bigger one. "I'll take you out in a minute." They both licked her hand.

A feeling of contentment swept over her. For the first time in her life, she actually felt as if she belonged somewhere. That she was wanted, not an inconvenience. That she had something to give. She didn't know a lot, but with time, she would learn. If Grant would keep her on after her debt was paid.

She liked her job. The constant challenge of dealing with the pets and their owners kept her on her toes.

When she'd first started, she hadn't been too sure about her role at the clinic, or how well she'd fit in.

Grant had welcomed her, and his niece, Amanda, treated her with kindness too. Only his aunt, Mrs. Thatcher, treated her coolly. She couldn't figure the older woman out and didn't necessarily want to. She reminded her of one of the social workers assigned to her when she was a child.

She smiled, contented, but wondered how Grant would feel about her today after her confessions last night. Between her customers, she'd gone over the scene in her head. Relived it in fact, even down to the last moments in his arms. Instead of shying away, she'd enjoyed his hug. It brought back images of a lost time when her mother, on a good day, would comfort her, before the bitter reality of the bottle hit.

Yet, it was different. The rhythmic beat of Grant's heart, his comforting words, and the scent of soap mingled with musky aftershave was nothing like the sweet, sickening smell of gin or the slurred words produced by the liquor.

No. Grant was sincere and she wouldn't have done anything to stop him had he tried to kiss her, but he hadn't. She sighed. Obviously, he didn't find her the least bit attractive. It had never bothered her before, but now she cursed her red hair and freckles as she headed to the front of the clinic.

Though in a way, it was probably better he didn't pursue her. Sarah needed to keep her distance so she wouldn't get hurt again, and suppressed that familiar sense of longing that had accompanied her everywhere lately.

"Grant? Rocky? I'm here."

Her dog barreled out of Grant's office with her boss not too far behind. Grant, dressed in his white lab coat, worn over a red polo shirt and khaki pants, looked unusually handsome today.

Sarah's breath caught in her throat as she slipped on her own lab coat before Rocky jumped up and licked her face. "Hi, baby." Scratching him behind his ears, she planted a big kiss on his nose. Then she gave Grant a tentative smile. "Hi."

"Hi, Sarah."

His smile didn't reach his eyes. He gave her a searching look, but didn't say anything as he shoved his hands into his coat pocket. Sarah's fingers bunched the fur behind Rocky's ears as her spirits dropped. He continued to lick her face as his tail wagged furiously behind him.

At least someone was glad to see her. It was at times like this that Sarah was glad she'd adopted him. He always made her feel good. After a final pat, she settled him on the floor and took a deep breath to steady her voice. "What needs to get done today?"

The jingle of bells sounded as the front door opened. Sarah stepped out from the back, the broom still in her hand. Grant was checking on the dog he'd done surgery on this morning, and Mrs. Thatcher had left early complaining of a headache.

"Can I help you?" she asked the woman who'd obviously been here before. She'd walked right past the reception area and straight into Grant's office.

The familiarity the stranger gave off confused Sarah. In her weeks of working here, she'd never seen her, nor heard Grant or Mrs. Thatcher talk about her. Yet somehow, she looked familiar and seemed to belong.

"Sure. Where's Grant?"

The woman turned around and Sarah realised this was one of the women from the photographs she'd seen on Grant's desk. She shrunk inwardly at the woman's striking beauty. The photo didn't do her justice, nor show how tall and thin she was.

Any feelings Sarah had for him dried up. Embarrassment surged through her. Silly of her to think Grant's actions were anything more than employer to employee.

"He's in the back. I'll go get him for you." Sarah wanted to grab Rocky and run. Had Grant's girlfriend found out he was at her apartment? Did she come to have it out with Grant? Or her?

"Don't bother. He'll know I'm here soon enough. You must be Sarah." The way she looked at her made Sarah want to shrink in her skin further. Surely she didn't see her as an obstacle.

"I'm Gillian. Sorry I haven't come sooner, but I was

stuck in LA on business. I've looked forward to meeting you." The smile on her lips didn't match the cool look in her eyes as she extended her hand.

Sarah shook it, not wanting to offend the woman, although touching her was the last thing she wanted to do. "Gillian?"

More confusion set in as the woman settled herself in Grant's chair, picked up her picture and stared at it a second before dusting it with her sleeve. "Grant hasn't told you about me?"

Sarah's heart did a somersault but she couldn't blame anyone but herself. Grant hadn't asked her to fall in love with him. In fact, he'd given no indication that he cared for her in any other way than as an employer. It was simply her own silly daydreams and longings that should have stayed buried. She stood frozen to the spot just shy of the desk, as Grant appeared.

"Hi, Gillian. I heard you all the way in the back room and came as quickly as possible before you ate Sarah alive with your questions. What haven't I told her?"

"Who I am. Are you ashamed of me?"

"Hardly." Sweeping the woman into his arms, he planted a kiss on her cheek. "You always have perfect timing, Gillian. I see the film wrapped early. How'd it go?"

"Just fine. The usual problems with actors with big egos, but now that I'm back, I had to stop by and meet your new assistant. So be a dear and introduce us properly."

Grant looked at Gillian, then at her. Uncomfortable with the whole situation, Sarah was ready to bolt even though she was tired of running. Accusations from an earlier time echoed in her mind. The circumstances were different, but then she'd been able to make a clean break. Here it wouldn't be quite so easy. She had Rocky to think of, not to mention school, the diner, or her unpaid bill.

"Gillian Morrison, Sarah Churchill. Sarah, my beloved pain-in-the-neck twin sister, Gillian, makeup artist to the stars."

Sarah felt the color rise on her cheeks. Now that she took a long, close look at the woman, she wondered how she could have missed the family resemblance. Gillian had the same coloring and bone structure as her brother.

"Pleased to meet you, Gillian." Relieved and a bit embarrassed because she jumped to conclusions, Sarah took the other woman's hand in hers again and shook it soundly. The firmness of her handshake reminded Sarah of Grant, and how his hand had caressed her back last night. The color on her cheeks rose again at the memory.

"Hi, Sarah. It's nice to meet you too. I hope my brother has been treating you properly?" Gillian's coolness faded.

Sarah relaxed. "Of course. Your brother is one of the kindest, most generous people I've ever met."

A look Sarah couldn't read passed between his sister and Grant. "I know. That's why we all look out for him."

Gillian gave her a warm smile. It was as if Sarah had been put through a test and passed it. Then she faced her brother. "Mom wants you to stop by tonight to discuss the barbecue this weekend. Oh and get a haircut, the shaggy look doesn't become you." She pulled on a stray piece of Grant's hair and turned to Sarah. "Men. If it weren't for us women, nothing would ever get done. You'll bring Sarah along Sunday, won't you?"

Grant gazed at her. Sarah didn't know what to say. The faraway look she'd seen earlier had disappeared; replaced by an intense one that made her toes curl. Had her earlier conclusion been wrong?

"It's just a barbecue with the family. Please come," Gillian raid to her as she slung her purse strap over her shoulder.

"Yes. Please say you'll come," Grant echoed softly.

Overwhelmed by the invitation, Sarah agreed to go. It was only a day with a few of his family. How hard could it be?

Chapter Seven

A few people turned out to be 50, of all ages and sizes. Sarah sat mortified at one of the many picnic tables set up around the yard as Grant went in search of some soda. She should have brought Rocky along. Large family gatherings had never been a favorite pastime of hers; she'd always felt inadequate, invisible among the people who'd taken her in.

The urge to run ate at her as she clutched her light-weight sweater together to keep out the cool air as the sun disappeared behind a cloud. Indian summer was over; fall had made its appearance last night. She shivered, wishing she'd brought her jacket.

Grant should have returned by now with her drink, but obviously he'd been detained by one of his many relatives. Sarah dug her nails into the palms of her hands. The only thing that kept her here was her pride, and the knowledge that it would hurt Grant if she disappeared.

It wasn't that she didn't know anybody. Grant had made sure to introduce her to several people on the way in but all the faces jumbled together. Sarah would never remember any of these people once she left and so far, Gillian or Mrs. Thatcher had yet to appear.

Veronica spotted her and wove her way through the crowd toward her. "Hi, Sarah." She sat down on the opposite bench.

Surprised, Sarah gave her a timid smile. "Hi."

"I'm going out with Grant's brother, Matthew." She waved her hand at the assembled crowd. "It can be rather intimidating, can't it? You get used to it though. I grew up with most of them, and I still get some of the cousins confused. It just takes a while, that's all. Hi, Grant."

"Hi, Veronica." He sat down on the wood bench next to Sarah. She sighed in relief, even though his nearness did crazy things to her. It had since that first night in her apartment.

A surge of energy zapped her as their hands touched when he handed her the soda, and the intense longing flared again. Scared, it was all she could do to stay seated and not run away. But she was tired of running. That's why she settled in Greer in the first place.

"Sorry I took so long, I ran into a cousin I haven't seen for a while and couldn't get away." He rolled his eyes and gave her a sheepish grin. "Susan had to tell me all about her latest exploits—you'll understand when you meet her."

"It's okay. You don't have to apologize to me."

"But I do. It's rude to bring a guest and ignore her." She trembled as he reached to tuck a strand of hair that had escaped from her ponytail behind her ear. His touch reassured her, his voice blanketed her in a cocoon of warmth. "Especially when she hardly knows anyone."

"There's Matthew," Veronica broke in, and Sarah was glad for the distraction. Her emotions were spiraling out of control. "See you later." Veronica loped off toward what Sarah would consider a younger version of Grant, even down to the cropped, dark, wavy hair.

Sarah protested, not wanting Grant to guess her unease among his family. "I know a few people." She looked at him again, unsure if she liked his new hair cut. She'd grown accustomed to the way his curls lay over his collar in an unkempt fashion.

Long or short, she still found him incredibly attractive—and dangerous. A lethal combination since she wanted to—no, needed to—depend on no one but herself. Years of self-preservation demanded it. Still, she knew she'd found herself starting to rely on him, which could only end with a broken heart.

Sarah's hair tickled Grant's fingertips as he pushed it out of her face. The soft curls enticed him, her freckles enchanted him, her green eyes fascinated him. He wanted to feel her lips beneath his, drink in the essence of her. He'd had high hopes for today. From their few conversations when he'd gotten Sarah to talk, he realized that she had never known what a normal home life was like.

He'd wanted that to change.

He'd wanted her to feel comfortable around his family, to fit in. It was important to him. He'd begun to think too much about Sarah in ways that had nothing to do with her work at the clinic.

Now he wasn't sure this barbecue was such a great idea. His mother had gone overboard, inviting the whole clan. Grant sensed her discomfort, regardless of her words. "A few was the operative word, Sarah. I was expecting immediate family today, not every cousin, aunt and uncle, and person in between. I'm sorry."

"I'm okay, really."

He didn't contradict her. "I'm glad. Let me show you around the old homestead." Cupping his hand under her elbow, he helped her rise to her feet, then steered her toward the back of his parent's house. His grip tightened possessively around her arm as he avoided eye contact with everyone so they could proceed uninterrupted to the back door and into the kitchen.

"Well, this is it. The place where I grew up." Looking around the sunny kitchen, his mood lightened. He wondered if Sarah could sense the love, the happiness that surrounded them.

In every nook and cranny, some memory of an earlier time bombarded him; kitchen magnets he and Gillian made in summer camp secured newspaper clippings of some Morrison activities, a ceramic soap dish in the shape of a frog made by his brother Matthew sat on the windowsill, and his mother's frilly, white apron hung from a peg by the refrigerator.

"We used to help my mom make chocolate chip cookies over there." He pointed to the counter by the far wall. "And we used to eat them over at the table, with a glass of milk after school while we did our homework."

"You don't strike me as much of a baker." Sarah looked at him, her green eyes widening slightly. Her jaw slackened and a slight smile played at her lips.

"There's a lot you don't know about me, my dear." He was glad to see some of the tension had dissipated. "Of course, I should clarify that we didn't actually bake all the dough. Most of it ended up in our stomachs. Back then we didn't worry that raw eggs could make us sick."

"Raw? I've never eaten raw cookie dough before."

"No? Well, you're in for a treat." Grant walked over to the freezer, opened the door and pulled out a roll of dough wrapped in wax paper in a freezer bag. "My mother makes a bunch at a time so all she has to do is slice and bake when the grandkids come over."

Reaching down, he pulled a knife out of the drawer and cut the roll. "Don't tell her I'm doing this. She'll have my head for spoiling your appetite." He divided the piece in two, handed one to Sarah, and then popped the other half into his mouth. "A little hard, but as good as always. What do you think?"

The look on Sarah's face enchanted him. Excitement replaced surprise, which replaced apprehension. "Wow. That's good. Would your mother notice if we ate more?"

"Of course, mothers know everything." As soon as the words slipped out, Grant knew he'd made a mistake. Her expression, so open before, shut down tighter than Fort Knox. He cursed himself for bringing up the subject. He was trying to make Sarah forget about her past and all he'd succeeded in doing was to remind her. "Let's go. I'll give you a quick tour of the rest of the house."

He placed the dough back in the freezer, and steered her through the old two-story farmhouse and out the front door. He had more things to show Sarah, and with any luck he might be able to make her forget about her childhood.

A more likely scenario was that it would only show her what she missed, but it was a chance he had to take. Somebody had to show her what it meant to be a family.

"Where are we going? The party's out back."

"I wanted to show you one of my special spots."

Keeping her by his side, he escorted her past the old barn, which now doubled as the garage and storage area, toward a huge oak tree growing near the property line. A well-worn tractor tire hung from one of the lower limbs. Fortunately, none of his nieces or nephews were around.

"A tire swing?" Sarah walked up to the rubber tire and ran her hand across the faded black surface. "I've always wanted to swing on one. It's safe?"

Grant tugged on the thick piece of rope. "Of course. My dad checks it every spring to make sure everything is okay. Here, let me help you get in." Stepping up behind her, he grabbed Sarah around the waist and lifted her. The sweet, herbal scent of her shampoo drifted by his nose as her ponytail swung in his face. He longed to loosen the darned thing and run his fingers through her curls, but the impropriety stopped him. Both Sarah, and certain members of his family, would probably take offense to the action. "Take hold of the rope and slip your legs into the hole."

Sarah did as Grant suggested, disappointed when he released his hold. She enjoyed the protective warmth of his arms around her, even though she tried to deny it.

As he began to push her, she appreciated his trying to make her feel welcome among his family, but the emotional scars from years of neglect could not be healed overnight. Nor did she want them to. They formed a defensive layer to keep her from being hurt again although it was probably too late. She was in love with her boss.

Four screaming kids broke the silence as they rounded the corner of the barn, running as fast as their legs could carry them. "Not it," the older boy yelled as he tagged the tree, followed by two other boys.

The smallest one, a girl, whom Sarah vaguely recalled belonged to a cousin on Grant's mother's side, wobbled up last. "Not it." She slapped the tree with her tiny hand.

"But you are, Jordan. You're last. Catch us if you can," shouted the boy in a green T-shirt. They took off running, leaving the confused girl standing by the tree.

"Wait for me," Jordan cried.

As Sarah looked at the child, a lump formed in her throat. She knew how the girl felt. Maybe Grant's family wasn't as perfect as he wanted her to believe, although these boys weren't as cruel as her foster siblings had been in home number two, nor had Sarah been quite so young.

She fought the memories of a long time ago. Their taunts and jeers couldn't hurt her now unless she let them.

"Hey, Jordan, want to swing for a while?" Grant knelt beside the sobbing child and wrapped his arms around her. Sarah's mood lifted as he occupied the girl's attention.

" 'Kay. Can I?"

"Of course, sweetheart. As long as you're with a grownup, it'll be okay." He lifted the girl and placed her on Sarah's lap. "You remember Sarah don't you?"

The girl shook her head, settling her small body against her. Sarah wrapped an arm around her. "I'm a friend of your Uncle Grant's. How old are you?"

Jordan held out three fingers.

"Wow, you're a big girl. Can you help me hold onto the tire so we don't fall off? I hear your uncle can push us into the next county if we're not careful."

Jordan giggled. Holding her securely, Sarah felt giddy herself as Grant pulled the tire back to get the momentum going again. He pushed them so high Sarah thought they were going to touch the fluffy, white clouds in the sky. The child's laughter mingled with her own.

Sarah's loosely tied ponytail came undone and she could feel her hair whipping around her face with each swing. Getting the tangles out would be hard, but the ride was worth it. She couldn't recall ever feeling so happy. Her spirits stayed buoyant even after the ride ended.

"You girls have worn me out," Sarah heard Grant pant as the swing stopped. "I suppose we should join the family before they wonder what happened to us."

He helped them out, then picked up their discarded soda cans before they headed to the backyard, Jordan running along in front of them. "I meant to tell you the other night, you look good with your hair down, you should wear it that way more often."

Sarah squirmed under Grant's gaze but made no comment as she put her hair tie into her jeans pocket. She'd always hated her curly, red hair. It had been impossible to style, but she'd never thought about cutting it off, so she'd always worn it back.

"There you are," Gillian called out, waving at them to join her as they rounded the side of the house. "Come on, Grant, come on, Sarah. We need two more on our team so we can beat the pants off the Blake family." She stood among six other people who, if she remembered correctly, were Grant's oldest sister, Patty and her husband Bob, his older sister, Caroline and her husband Richard, his younger brother, Matthew, and Veronica.

"Let's go." Grant pulled her over to where Gillian stood. "It's a game of volleyball. We do it every year. The losers have to do a beer run."

Sarah hesitated. "I thought you were tired."

"Not for a quick game."

"But I don't know how to play."

"Do you think we do? Come on, it's fun. The worst that can happen is I run to Walt's and buy a case. All you have to do is hit the ball over the net and don't let it go out of bounds."

Which was easier said than done. Even after a few minutes of practice, Sarah wasn't quite sure what was going on or how much she'd help the team. Fortunately, most of the time the ball sailed over her head or fell closer to someone else.

Eventually, it sailed right toward her. Sarah squeezed her eyes shut, put her arms together like Grant had shown her and swung. The ball stung as it connected with her skin. She didn't dare look at where the ball went until she heard triumphant shouts from her teammates.

"You did it, Sarah." Veronica ran over and gave her a big hug. "Right over Jeremy's head. That'll teach you to be so cocky," she yelled over her shoulder at the gawky teenager who'd turned beet red from the ribbing.

Sarah felt sorry for him for a moment, until she realized that the jokes were made out of love, not out of cruelty. She'd never known there was a difference before.

She almost felt like one of the family.

The dinner bell sounded, signaling an end to the match. Thanks to Sarah, the Morrison side was ahead, so Grant's cousin left to go to Walt's. Sarah was glad the game was over. She doubted she'd be able to make another great shot, even if it was a match to determine who bought the beer.

"Nice job, Sarah." Patty gave her a high-five.

Richard followed. "You can be on our team anytime."

"Looks like you're the hit of the afternoon," Grant declared, escorting her to the table loaded with food.

"I'm not sure I'd go that far." Sarah's mouth watered as she looked at the burgers, baked beans, salads, chips and of course, chocolate chip cookies.

They loaded their plates and sat down at one of the many tables set about the yard. Sarah kept close to Grant's side, which wasn't a problem since table space was hard to find. She could hardly concentrate on the food with Grant's thigh touching hers in such an intimate way as she sat wedged between him and his cousin, Susan, who was just as interesting as he'd promised.

Dressed in a long, gauzy, flowered skirt, topped by an oversized red sweater, complete with cowboy boots and hat, the blond screamed of eccentricity.

"So you're Sarah. Hi. I'm Susan, the family fruitcake." Her laughter resembled the tinkling of a wind chime. "I've heard you're Grant's new assistant. It's about time he got himself some decent help. I would have volunteered myself, but I'm allergic to anything that requires feeding. What else do you do?"

The woman was like a whirlwind. Sarah liked her but had a hard time following the conversation. "I go to school, work at Greer's Diner and Grant's clinic."

"Goodness! You're one busy beaver. I do as little as possible. You might call me the black sheep of the family. I dabble in the arts, you know, painting, sculpting, papier-maché, what ever medium I feel like at that moment."

"Do you make any money?"

"Heavens no. Where do you think the term starving artist came from?"

As she bounced from story to story, Sarah knew she'd never met anyone quite like the forty-something woman beside her. Not even the homeless people with whom she'd shared meals and fires could compete with her tales. Next to Susan, Sarah's life didn't seem quite so unusual.

"I love her, Grant. Bring her by the studio, I'd like to paint her—that's the medium I'm into these days. A closed azalea, a little frostbitten around the edges, waiting to burst open and reveal her warm inner self." She patted Sarah on the cheek as she rose from the bench. "Ta-ta, so many relatives, so little time. See you around."

A sigh escaped Sarah's lips as Susan flitted off to engage another relative in lively conversation. "Wow."

"Now you see why I took so long in bringing you the soda earlier. Come on. I'll introduce you to some of my normal cousins after you meet Aunt Mildred."

Grant led her to a thin woman dressed in black, sitting on a foldout lawn chair, and leaned over to kiss the weathered cheek, colored with a hint of red rouge. "Aunt Mildred, meet Sarah Churchill. Sarah, meet Aunt Mildred. Aunt Mildred's the matriarch of the Morrison clan. She's into her nineties, and nothing happens without her knowing. Even I get the crack of her whip." Grant had on a mischievous smile.

"Hello, Sarah. It's nice to meet you." His aunt

pointed a gnarled finger at Grant. "Watch your tongue, boy, or I'll tell your friend all your deep, dark secrets."

"It's nice to meet you too." Sarah guessed the old lady was joking because she winked at her. Maybe she wasn't the only one with something in their past to hide. Though with the family support Grant had, she couldn't imagine it was anything like her own.

They spent the next few hours in conversation with just about everyone there. Before, she'd always felt like a spectator, but today, it was as if the Morrison clan had wanted her to be here, to be a part of them. They'd accepted her as Grant's friend and assistant.

The party broke up after sunset, and much to Sarah's relief, Grant declined the invitation to continue the festivities at the local bar. They found his parents in the driveway, waving goodbye to a distant cousin and his family. Sarah made her farewells. "I had a great time, John, Olivia. Thanks for inviting me."

She liked them both immensely. His father, an older version of Grant, right down to the deep blue eyes, was quiet and reserved. While his mother, petite with white hair, always had a welcoming smile on her lips. The image of her in the kitchen, in a dress, wearing a white apron, baking chocolate chip cookies invaded her thoughts. Olivia was the type of mother Sarah had always wanted when she still believed in dreams.

Maybe she'd never really outgrown them.

Sarah shuddered. Her thoughts were impossible.

"Can you give my good-byes to the rest of the family?"

"Of course, dear. It was nice meeting you too." Grant's mother gave her a hug, and his father, a firm handshake. "Stop by and visit any time. You don't need to wait until Grant brings you."

An easy silence prevailed in the short drive back to her apartment. Sarah was tired. She leaned her head against the seat and shut her eyes, listening to the soft jazz on the radio.

Back at her building, Sarah debated on whether to invite Grant inside until she saw Mrs. Maddox draw the curtains back in her apartment downstairs. She decided against it. She couldn't handle anything else today.

"Thanks, Grant. I had a—an interesting time."

"You're welcome." As he leaned in, she closed her eyes just like she'd seen in the movies and waited. Anticipation mixed with caution. But instead of kissing her senseless, his lips brushed hers then retreated. "You were the hit of the day. See you Monday."

Embarrassed at her own presumptions, Sarah bounded from the car and flew up the stairs, hoping to avoid her nosy neighbor. As promised, Lorraine had stopped by to take Rocky out, but she hadn't been able to prevent him from chewing up her favorite pair of shoes.

Sarah sank down in the middle of the floor.

"Rocky, you bad dog! I thought we cured you of

this?" she scolded him, holding up her black flats, which now had the bow chewed off the left one, and the slight heel of the right one almost completely gone.

Tired and overcome by the day's events, she threw the shoes into the corner before she crawled onto her daybed and hugged the pillow. Too many emotions swirled around her, threatening to shatter the wall she'd built around her heart. All because of one man. Grant.

Rocky slunk toward her, his tail down. He nuzzled his snout against her and licked her face. Sarah hugged his big, furry body and cried. Rocky still loved her, even after she yelled at him, and Grant had only been too happy to introduce her to his family. Maybe all these years she'd been wrong.

Maybe she was lovable after all.

Chapter Eight

"Hi Sarah, what are you looking for?" Lindsay Morrison asked her as she stood in the aisle of the Goodwill store in Denton. "I'm shopping for old seventies duds. There's a theme party at school Saturday night."

Horrified, Sarah stared at Grant's niece. Aside from the coat Grant had given her and personal items, she hadn't owned anything new in years. She was here to replace the black shoes Rocky had chewed and to find clothes to wear to night school, not some costume for a dance. Humiliation stained her cheeks. She couldn't believe her luck at seeing a member of Grant's family. What were the odds?

"I—I—"

In the nick of time, Grant's older sister swung

around the corner with a cart in tow. "Yoohoo, girls, have I got some stuff for you. Hi, Sarah, nice to see you again. Have you recovered from the party yet?"

"Y–yes, hi," she stammered, trying to recall her name. She drew a blank.

The other woman must have sensed her hesitation. "It's Caroline, but I hardly expect you to remember with all the relatives Grant subjected you to last weekend. It's amazing you survived at all, especially once Aunt Mildred got a hold of you. She can be a bit bothersome."

Sarah blushed. She'd liked Grant's aunt. She'd reminded her of a thin version of her long ago neighbor, Mrs. White. "Aunt Mildred's a kind, sweet woman."

"Oh, she is. Don't get me wrong, but she can be set in her ways." Caroline turned and sorted through the rack of clothes directly in front of her. "Let's just say we don't always see eye to eye with her. Wow, will you look at this?" Grant's sister grabbed a pair of purple bell-bottom pants. "Hard to believe these actually came back in style."

Sarah never paid attention to style and fads, but even she had to admit the flared trousers were loud, though she did like the color. "They are a bit much, aren't they?"

"Yes, and unfortunately, some of us were around to wear this stuff the first time. I can't imagine . . ." She pulled out a monstrous lime-green leisure suit jacket from the cart and held it up to her chest. "Lindsay,

Allison, don't you think this will look adorable on cousin Jeremy?"

The girls squealed their agreement as they continued to search the racks for something suitable.

"I don't know, Mom. All this stuff is so ugly." Lindsay grabbed a pink, polyester blouse complete with frills and laughed. "Who in their right mind would ever wear something like this? Are you sure we'll find what we're looking for?"

"Lindsay Marie Patterson, I taught you better manners than that. Obviously at one time, someone thought it was perfectly fine. Now you two go over there and continue your search. I want to talk to Sarah." After putting the blouse back on the rack, Caroline waited until the girls were on the other side of the aisle before she continued. "So you're taking classes at Denton Community College. What are you studying? I never had a chance to ask."

"Just general education right now. I haven't decided on a major yet."

"I envy you. I never continued my education. I married Richard right out of high school. He was my sweetheart." Caroline sighed. "He still is. Anyway, that's all in the past. What's important is right here and now, don't you think?"

Sarah shifted uncomfortably from one foot to the other. "Of course," she agreed, not wanting to elaborate on how the past affected her present life, especially with Grant's sister.

With a glance at her watch, Sarah knew she needed to continue looking; her afternoon off was passing quickly. She'd have to leave soon to get to her English class.

"Oh, don't let me keep you. I've got some looking to do myself. I'll see you later." Cart in tow, Caroline disappeared into the next aisle.

Sarah sighed in relief and kept examining the blouses, but her afternoon was ruined. Though she couldn't blame Caroline or Lindsay, she could only blame herself. By allowing Grant and his family into her life, she'd opened herself up to caring about their opinions.

Lost in thought, she didn't see Caroline return. "Hey Sarah, check this out. I bet it would look great on you." She pulled out a rose-colored silk blouse and held it up. "I can't believe someone would get rid of a perfectly good shirt. I wish it were my size."

The shirt was beautiful she had to admit, and so were the two others she showed her. "And look here." Caroline pulled out a cute vest with different types of dogs embroidered on it. "It's still got the tags on it. Go figure." She put all the clothes in Sarah's cart.

"And I did find this for myself." She held up a beautiful black cocktail dress with a scooped neck and long slender sleeves. "I have a dinner engagement through Richard's work next weekend. Why spend a fortune on something I'll probably wear once?"

Sarah nodded her agreement, figuring Grant's sister

was only trying to make her feel better. She appreciated the thought, but couldn't voice the words. Escape was her only option, as usual.

"Come on, let's go try the clothes on."

"I'm sure everything will fit. I've gotta run, or I'll be late for class. Please say good-bye to the girls for me?" Sarah grabbed her cart and sped to the cashier.

The bell signaled a new arrival. Sarah hurried to the front. Mrs. Thatcher had left to run a few errands and Grant was in his office on a conference call with another vet, trying to figure out what was the matter with Mrs. O'Leary's cat.

Sarah could have told him it was probably just a case of nerves. The darned feline had made the mistake of chasing an ornery, old crow and the bird had taken to dive bombing the cat every time it went outside. But what did she know? Grant was the expert.

"May I help you?"

"Hi, Sarah." Gillian turned away from the display of dog food piled along the far wall. "I was hoping you'd be here today. I have some things for you. Can you sneak out for a few minutes, or is that brother of mine a slave driver?"

Gillian's appearance surprised her. She brushed away some dog hair stuck to her lab coat. "No. He's not. I just finished cleaning up in back. I'm sure I can leave for a moment or two. Let me leave a note."

Gillian led the way to her little red sports car. Somehow it fit Grant's sister. Grant too, if he chose to drive a car instead of a van. Of the two, Grant's vehicle was more practical, but Gillian's looked like more fun.

"Want to take it for a spin?"

She'd love to, but she knew she didn't belong in a car like that. So did the cops when they pulled her over while driving her foster sister's boyfriend's car. Sarah had had no clue the car hadn't been borrowed from a friend. Fortunately, she'd gotten off on a technicality, but the event had left its mark, as had all the others. "No. Maybe some other time. I've still got a lot to do. Thanks for the offer though."

"No problem. Here." The trunk popped open when Gillian released the latch. She handed Sarah the plastic bag inside. "Caroline and I were going through our closets the day after she met you at Goodwill and thought you might like these. You're such a tiny thing, though, you'll probably need to alter them."

Sarah went rigid, the smile frozen on her face. A wave of humiliation coursed through her. She should have known something like this would happen the minute she saw Caroline and her daughters in the store.

Hand-me-downs. The very words struck at the center of her heart. She could still hear the taunts, the jeers of her foster sisters and their friends.

> *Sarah, Sarah, carrot top,*
> *Always gets what we don't*
> *want.*

Don't matter if it's big or small,
Sarah, Sarah wears it all.

It was one thing to buy clothes at a resale shop. The faces of those who wore them before were anonymous. But to accept things from Grant's family—his sisters—was more than Sarah could handle. Every time she wore something of theirs, she could only imagine the looks and stares she'd receive. She was not a charity case.

Gillian must have seen her expression. "Hey, look. I'm sorry. We didn't mean to offend you. We're always trading clothes. Since these things were too small for both of us, we thought you might like them. But if you don't want them, that's okay. I'll just donate them to the church rummage sale."

Hurt flashed through Gillian's eyes. In that instant, Sarah realized Grant's sisters were only trying to help, not make fun of her. And Sarah had thrown their generosity back in Gillian's face. When was she going to learn that the Morrisons weren't like any other family she'd ever encountered? That their actions were sincere, based on kindness, not out of spite or malice?

She swallowed her pride and managed with as much grace as she could muster, "No. I'm not offended. I'm sure they're beautiful things. Better than I could find at the thrift store. Thanks. I'll get a lot of use out of them."

Retreating to the clinic with the large black, garbage bag in hand, Sarah's heart was ready to burst. Maybe the time had come to let go of the past, and embrace the present and all Grant and his family had to offer— if Grant could quit thinking about her as his assistant. The idea scared her, and excited her at the same time.

"What was Gillian doing here?" Grant appeared in the doorway of his office, his hair unkempt as if he'd been running his hand through it trying to solve a problem. Sarah ached to set it back in place, but her newfound emotions were too raw to contemplate such an action.

"She stopped by to give me some things," Sarah whispered, overcome by a fierce passion. She'd fallen in love with not only Grant, but his entire family as well. The family she'd always wanted. The family that had always been just out of reach. Maybe she'd finally found them.

Then she did something she hadn't done for a long time. She bent her head and cried. For years she'd buried her emotions deep. Nobody had ever paid attention before, nobody had ever cared, nobody had ever given her reason to—until Grant and his family.

Grant sprung from the doorway. "Hey! What's wrong?" He gathered Sarah in his arms, surprised and encouraged when she didn't stiffen at the contact. Cradling her head in the crook of his shoulder, he rocked her gently as her tears saturated his lab coat. "Shhh. Everything's okay."

But everything wasn't okay. Grant knew that as soon as he put his arms around her again. The feelings she'd been evoking since he met her came crashing back with such force, Grant was breathless.

The fierce desire to protect Sarah overwhelmed him. What had his aunt said about him saving the world? Right now, he only wanted to save Sarah from whatever demons plagued her.

He knew she'd grown up without family, but there was still so much mystery about her. Too much he didn't know but wanted to. If only she'd let him in. Gently, he rubbed the small of her back and caressed the top of her head with his cheek until Rocky wedged his way in between them, silencing his questions.

Grant released Sarah and moved away as she sank to the floor and buried her face into the dog's coat, her fingers grasping at the curls. Rocky managed to wriggle around until he could lick the moisture from her cheeks. For a moment, Grant stood there, unsure of what to do. He wanted to comfort her, but to his disappointment, she wanted her dog, not him.

As Sarah's tears subsided, fierce hiccups racked her body. "Here." He handed her a tissue he'd retrieved from Aunt Mary's desk. "I'll get you something to drink."

He returned with a cup of cool water and watched with impatient fascination as she drank. The slender arch of her neck was made for kissing, her hair the right texture to weave his fingers through, her body soft and pliable to mold against his. An ache to hold her again coursed through him.

"Thanks. I—I'm sorry. I owe you an explanation." Her throaty voice encircled him and drove him to the edge. One more step and he'd be beyond saving. "I'm not used to such kindness. When I was in one of my foster homes they used to give me things when the social worker visited. Then, once they left, they would take them back and give them to their own children, while I got nothing but unwanted leftovers."

No matter how much Grant wanted to know, he was not ready for her story. The truth knifed him in the gut. "What?"

He tilted her head back and gazed into her green-flecked eyes filled with hurt and longing. He brushed away the remaining tears from her cheeks. The comment she'd made weeks ago finally made sense. "So that's why it's so hard for you to accept things. Don't worry. No one's ever going to take anything or make you feel bad again."

He wanted to kiss her, to chase away her hurt, her fears, but he knew it wouldn't be a light peck on the lips, and his next appointment would be in any minute. Not only was Mrs. Huebner punctual, she was also his aunt's best friend and another busybody.

"Hi, stranger," her neighbor greeted her Thursday afternoon as Sarah locked her bike to the lamppost outside their apartment building.

"Hi, Lorraine. How are you?" Sarah grabbed a bag of groceries from the basket, feeling a little guilty. She hadn't spoken to her friend all week. Not even to thank her for walking Rocky last weekend.

Lorraine, like herself, was from the Bay area and another outsider to Greer, which was probably why they got along so well. Friendships were hard for Sarah to establish anyway, and doubly hard in such a close-knit community.

"I'm fine. I finally dumped that creep, Adam. Here, let me help you." Lorraine pulled out the other bag and settled it on her hip. "When do I get to meet your man? Where've you been hiding him, and does he have any *single* friends?"

Sarah shifted uncomfortably in her jean jacket. She'd never mentioned Grant to Lorraine. Her friend must have seen him drop her off last night with her pile of new clothes. But rides, a few dinners, and meeting his family didn't mean a thing. He hadn't shown any other interest in her, at least not in the way she'd seen it in the movies. "He's not my man, he's my boss."

"Honey, what planet do you come from?" Lorraine tapped her on the shoulder with her long, acrylic nail. "Any man who brings his employee home after work, and helps her with her dog is more than a boss. He's nuts about you; I can see it in his eyes, even from a distance. And that is just what I'm looking for. Now let's get inside so I can see that big, black, hunk of male Rocky again. Maybe he's got a single friend too."

As Lorraine led the way up the three flights of steps, Sarah followed perplexed. What did Lorraine mean that Grant was nuts about her? He certainly hadn't given any indication of it.

Or had he?

Sarah slid the key into the lock and pushed the door open. Rocky barreled into her, glad to see her even though she'd only been gone an hour. "Hi, sweetie. I missed you too." She rubbed his favorite spot behind his ear with her free hand. "Look who's here to see you. Now let me put these groceries away. I have a treat for you."

"Hello, Rocky!" Her neighbor managed to set the bag down on the floor inside the door before he jumped all over her. "How's my big boy?"

Setting her bag on the counter, Sarah went to re-trieve Lorraine's, knowing she'd be occupied with Rocky for a while. Maybe she should convince her friend to go to the no-kill shelter and find a pet for herself. Since Rocky had come into her life, things had definitely improved.

"So, what's he like?" Lorraine joined her in the tiny kitchen, Rocky at her heels. Sarah pulled out the raw-hide bone she'd purchased and handed it to him. Rocky immediately sat down on the floor and began chewing away.

"Who? Grant?"

"Aha, so he has a name."

"Of course. Grant Morrison. My boss." Though even to her ears, that last sentence didn't sound very convincing. "He's kind and gentle and—"

"You're in love with him, aren't you?"

"No!" Having finished putting the groceries away, Sarah whirled around to find Lorraine blocking her path into the other room, a frown on her face. Sarah hung her head, her honest answer barely more than a whisper. "Yes."

"That's better. What are you going to do about it?"

"There's nothing *to* do about it. No matter what you think, Grant doesn't see me that way."

Lorraine stepped out of her way as Sarah ran to the bathroom, but appeared behind her as she stared at herself in the mirror. "Why should he? My hair is too messy, my face is too pale, my eyes are too wide, my lips too thin. And these freckles . . ." Sarah tried to scrub them off with a towel. "No wonder Grant doesn't look at me. I'm a freak."

"That's not what I see." As Lorraine gathered Sarah's hair so it appeared to be shoulder length, Sarah stared, transfixed. The style suited her. "With a decent haircut and a little makeup, you'd stop traffic, girl. Didn't anyone ever show you how to primp?"

Sarah shook her head. She supposed if she had wanted, one of her foster mothers might have explained things to her, but it hadn't been important then. And when she lived on the streets, a meal, a warm place to live, and staying out of jail were all she had time to think about.

But that was in the past. She'd wanted to make a change in her life, that's why she settled in Greer. She was in school to better her education, so why not better her looks while she was at it. All she had to do was ask. She swallowed her fear and met Lorraine's gaze in the mirror. "Can you show me?

"You bet. You know, when I get done with you, Grant won't be able to keep his paws off. He'll be another Rocky, slobbering all over you."

Comparing Grant to her dog alarmed her. Rocky never judged any of Sarah's actions, whether she was mad, upset, or happy. It had taken time, but she'd figured out that Rocky's love had no conditions no matter what she did, or had done before she found him. Would Grant be so understanding? "I've got a past I'm sure he wouldn't be too happy about."

"If Grant's the kind of man I think he is, he doesn't care about what you did, only what you do now. So let's take a look at your clothes."

"I hope you're right." Sarah sighed silently as she walked back into the main room. "Most of my clothes are in the closet, but there's a bag of stuff on the bed."

Lorraine plopped down on Sarah's daybed and pulled out a cream-colored blouse that Gillian had given her. "Honey, where did you get these things?" Next she held up a matching navy-blue suit with gold buttons down the front, then a short, black, tight skirt.

Sarah had been avoiding looking through the bag Gillian had given her. She'd just moved it from the daybed, to the floor, then back to the daybed when she left for work today. From what she could see, the clothes were gorgeous. Much better than anything she had ever owned. "Grant's sisters' gave them to me. I haven't had time to go through them."

As much as Sarah tried, she couldn't keep the edge from her voice even though she thought she'd come to terms with Gillian's gesture. Accepting things and reaching out were still hard for her to do, but she had to try. "They are beautiful, aren't they?"

"Look, Sarah. I don't know much about your past, and I won't ask any questions, but there is nothing wrong with accepting help from other people, whether it's emotional, financial, or clothes. Take me for example." Her laughter filled the studio apartment. "I'm always looking for a willing ear or someone to lean on. A person can't do everything by themselves. Now, I'm free tonight. Come over and I'll cut your hair and show you how to doll yourself up. Then we'll watch a chick flick while I paint your nails. I've got a new color that would look great on you. When I'm done, Grant won't know what hit him!"

At her silence, Lorraine questioned, "That is what you want, isn't it?"

A cloud of confusion washed over her. Sarah wasn't sure what she wanted anymore. Did she want really a solitary life, depending on or needing no one? The answer startled her.

No.

She wanted Grant to notice her, and hold her tight and love her for what she was.

Chapter Nine

Sarah heard the faint meowing over the steady drizzle of cold rain Friday morning. Pulling the collar of her coat tighter around her neck, she leaned her bike against the dumpster in the parking lot behind the clinic and followed the sound, Rocky at her side.

The high-pitched meow seemed softer now, more pitiful, more desperate, as she searched for the source. "Where are you, kitty?" The garbage bin was empty, as was the drainpipe and the discarded cardboard box nearby.

At five in the morning, the only light available shone from the pole overhead. She wished she had a flashlight, or at least the headlight from her bike, but the batteries had died again on her way to the clinic this morning. Grant wouldn't be too happy if he knew she'd ridden most of the way in the dark, but she was a big girl and had taken care of herself most of her life.

The thought of Grant brought a smile to her lips despite the rain, which in the past few minutes had turned into a steady downpour. The heavy drops plastered her hair to her head and she had no doubt her mascara was running down her cheeks. So much for her new look, but that was the least of her problems. She had to find the kitten.

"Where do you suppose he is Rocky?" He cocked his head as he looked at her, his ears raised ever so slightly in an inquisitive sort of way. Sarah swore he understood everything she said to him as she reached out to pat his damp head. "Can you find the kitty?"

Some scent or sound must have caught his attention because he darted off, nose to the ground, straight to the back door of the clinic. A shoe box with holes punched in the top had been left off to the side.

"Good boy." Sarah knelt down, almost afraid to open the rectangular box, but Rocky pawed at the top. From inside, Sarah could hear the pitiful moan of the kitten. Gently, she lifted the lid to reveal a tiny fluff of orange half-hidden in an old scrap of material. "You poor thing."

She reached in and stroked its head. The kitten cried out again. Rocky stuck his head in the box and sniffed at the scrawny bundle of fur, his nose almost as big as the kitten's head. Then to Sarah's surprise, he began to lick it. The kitten meowed feebly.

Sarah's tears mingled with the rain. Someone had abandoned the kitten. She knew exactly how the little animal felt to be left alone and frightened, wondering what was going to happen next.

Memories of the day the State stepped in surfaced. For a week, she'd been living alone in that two-room mobile home, eating stale bread and cold beans. She'd even managed to get herself to school because it hadn't been uncommon for her parents to disappear for a day or two. Except this time they never returned, and it took the overburdened State days to find her.

Mrs. White had done her best to take care of her and console her, but even her neighbor couldn't stop the social worker from ripping Sarah from her arms and transporting her to a strange neighborhood and family. And that hadn't happened just once, but six times, not counting the times she'd run away and been brought back by the police.

She shuddered as a cold drop of rain slid under her collar and chilled her skin. Sarah would make sure this tiny fella wouldn't experience anything quite as dramatic. As carefully as possible, she opened her jacket and shirt underneath and bundled it against her. Then she went to retrieve the keys to open the back door.

Once inside, she had no clue what to do. Removing her jacket, she pulled the kitten from beneath her shirt and placed it on the examining table. The poor thing sat huddled, shivering from the cold. Immediately, Sarah picked it up and took it to the back sink where she proceeded to give it a warm bath, then toweled it dry. Upon closer inspection, she figured the kitten couldn't be more than a few weeks old.

And very hungry.

She rummaged around the tiny refrigerator, looking for some milk, but came up empty handed. All she could find was a half-empty carton of creamer, so she diluted it with water and placed the saucer in front of her new charge.

The kitten sniffed at the liquid and turned away. Sarah ran to the bin where they kept cat food for the resident stray out back Grant hoped to trap and spay, and set a few bits on the table. Nothing. She even placed the food into the cream, but the kitten just stared at her.

Tears formed in her eyes again. If she couldn't get the kitten to eat, then it would die. And it would be all her fault. Just as everything always was when she was growing up. It didn't matter that she was a scared and lonely child, lost in a system supposed to provide for her. In every foster family, Sarah had been the scapegoat, the troubled one.

Clenching her hands into fists, Sarah shook her head to dispel those thoughts. She was not that helpless child anymore. Nor would she let her self-doubts overcome the years of self-discipline and her new found confidence. She had to do something.

And that something meant calling in sick to the restaurant so she could help the abandoned cat. Then, remembering Lorraine's advice from yesterday, she called Grant before she lost her nerve.

Startled from sleep, Grant could barely find the phone on the nightstand next to his bed. "This better be good," he mumbled to himself. The clock read 5:15 and Max and Matilda shifted from their sleeping positions at the foot of the bed.

"Morrison here."

"Grant? Did I wake you?" Sarah's voice at the other end of the line woke him instantly.

"Is something wrong?" He sat up in bed, displacing one of his cats, Boots, who had occupied the other pillow.

"No. Not really. The animals are fine. Rocky's fine. It's . . ." He heard the hesitation in her voice. "I'm sorry I woke you. I'll deal with it. Bye."

"Sarah, wait." The dial tone buzzed in his ear. He vaulted out of bed and headed straight for the shower, his morning jog on hold. He knew enough about Sarah to know the world could be ending before she'd ask anyone for help.

He arrived at the clinic in record time, glad that Greer's finest were probably eating. Charging through the back door, he stopped short, surprised to see Sarah bent over the examining table cooing softly. Shouldn't she have already left for the diner? Rocky sat patiently by her side, his tail thumping against the linoleum floor.

"What's wrong?"

Sarah turned at the sound of his voice. "You're here!" The surprise, mingled with pleasure, touched him as did the look of relief that flashed across her face. "You didn't need to come. I would've figured something out."

"But you shouldn't have to. I'm glad you called." Grant strode to the table. "What's the problem?" He eyed a kitten nestled in Sarah's hands. The orange feline barely filled her palm.

"Somebody left him by the back door."

"At least they had the sense to leave him here instead of the side of the road." Anger at the person who dumped the kitten coursed through him. Especially since it affected Sarah in such a way. She looked so vulnerable, so lost. And downright . . . beautiful. He sucked in a breath of damp air and took in her new look.

Her damp hair had been cut to her shoulders, creating a riot of waves that framed her face. Bangs, along with a dusting of eye shadow, some liner, and a coat of mascara, brought out the green in her eyes. Her lips shone with a hint of gloss. The old Sarah had had a raw beauty that intrigued him. The new Sarah was simply stunning.

Grant wanted to take her in his arms and hold her and not let go. Heck, he'd probably end up kissing her senseless. Then he'd really be in trouble because once he started, he doubted he'd be able to end it.

The kitten cried, breaking his train of thought.

"He's hungry. I don't know what to do. He won't eat the food I put out, nor drink any cream."

Grant picked up the ball of fluff, glad to see Sarah had kept it warm. The kitten was painfully thin, and no doubt hungry. A once over convinced him the kitten was healthy and a she. "Your kitten's a she, barely three weeks old and not weaned from her mother so she won't take regular food or milk yet. Not that you want to feed a kitten or cat milk or cream, they can't really digest it."

"Oh." Something like a look of chagrin crossed her features. "I'm glad she didn't eat what I tried to give her then, what do we do?"

Grant liked the way she included him in her problem. Whether Sarah realized it or not, she'd taken another big—no, giant—step in opening up to him. Smiling, he turned away and strode to the cabinets lined on the far wall.

"I keep this around for these types of emergencies." He pulled out a bottle of powdered formula and an eyedropper. "Mix this together, following the directions, then I'll show you how to feed her." The chime sounded on his watch. "It's five-thirty. If you don't have time, I can do it for you."

"I have time."

"Don't you have to work today?"

Sarah hung her head. "I called in sick. Veronica mentioned the other day she was looking for more hours so I suppose she'll be working mine."

"Are you sick?" Concern laced his voice though he tried to hide it. Sarah had been working a lot. Her schedule demanded it. Maybe he should cut back on her time here, seeing as her bill had almost been paid off, but he didn't like the idea of not seeing her almost every day.

"No."

Grant smiled at her, relieved. "Good. Glad to hear that. That means I can have you all day. I have a surgery scheduled for nine. With you here, it'll go much smoother."

He liked the idea of having Sarah with him the rest of the day. It would give him a chance to discover her plans for the future. He hoped they included staying in Greer.

After donning her surgical mask and gloves, Sarah lifted the gray tomcat out of the cage and handed him to Grant. "What's Gallahad in for today?"

"We're neutering him, so he won't sow his wild oats." She watched Grant place him in a glass container that reminded her of a fish tank. "And hopefully it'll keep him from spraying all over Mrs. Germaine's house."

"So why are you knocking him out this way instead

of using a shot?" Sarah adjusted the mask on her face to fit snugly over her nose and mouth.

"The recovery time is quicker." He fiddled with the knob to the tank that controlled the flow of gas. "He'll be out in a few minutes. Then we can start. Do you have any questions?"

Sarah shook her head. She had a ton of questions, but didn't know where to start. Most of her learning came from observations and reading anyway. Books had been her one solace growing up, and magazines and newspapers kept her current with world events as an adult.

"So tell me then, how long do you plan on staying in Greer?"

Sarah looked at Grant. The gentleness of his gaze loosened her lips and she found herself admitting things out loud she'd never said before. Grant had that affect on her. "I'm tired of running and living day to day. I promised to settle down when I found the right town. I think Greer's it."

Plus, Greer had Grant Morrison and his family—both accepting of her. She'd be crazy to leave.

"I'm happy to hear that." He moved a strand of loose hair from her face and placed it behind the strap of her mask with a simple caress. A tingling sensation coursed through her. "I forgot to mention how much I like your new hair style. It suits you."

Unused to compliments, Sarah was glad her mask hid the blush staining her cheeks as Grant turned away. She watched him lift the cat from the tank and set him on the metal table.

"Okay, here we go. Now place this over his nose and mouth."

He handed her a plastic mask, then stepped in behind her, his body mere inches from her own. Sarah could scarcely breathe with her own mask on and Grant's nearness made it even harder, but she forced herself to concentrate on the cat instead of him.

With his help, Sarah did as he instructed. Soon, excitement overruled her wildly beating heart at the prospect of seeing the procedure. So far, everything she'd helped with had been pretty routine.

Grant generally scheduled his surgeries in the mornings to allow ample time for recovery, usually while she was at Greer's Diner. A tinge of guilt swept through her, knowing she should be there right now, but Mabel could manage as long as Veronica was there.

"Good job. Now this machine keeps the oxygen flowing, as well as the gas that keeps him asleep." He pointed to a square contraption with a glass container filled with gray beads, a bag, dials and tubes. "If the cat stops breathing or goes into distress, we'll know immediately. Ready?"

At Sarah's nod, Grant quickly explained about the instruments lying on the tray he'd set up, then about the procedure. "Okay, here we go." In less than 10 minutes, he was done. They'd worked in perfect unison, which didn't surprise him one bit.

Grant was glad to see Sarah didn't flinch. Aunt Mary usually left as soon as she pulled out his instruments. If he had any doubts about the idea that formed in his brain, they fell by the wayside as Sarah stood calmly beside him during the entire surgery. Grant pulled the mask off his face. "You're good at this, you know. Have you thought about what you'll do once you finish the courses you're taking now?"

Grant had to know. It would be a big step for both of them and one he was crazy enough to take. With luck, Sarah would be as willing too. He trusted her, and if he didn't know better, he could swear that despite the fact that she was technically his employee, he'd fallen in love with her.

Sarah removed her own mask, then stroked the still-sleeping cat. Grant's words made her nervous. He had a habit of being able to draw responses from her that left her feeling open and vulnerable and more confused than ever. "I suppose I'll keep taking more classes until I have enough credits to transfer to a regular university."

"And what then? What will you study?"

"I don't know. I haven't really thought about it." At least not until now. Sarah never tried to think about anything in the long term because something always came up and she was on the move again.

He gave her a long searching look that quickened her pulse. "Maybe you should."

Sarah warmed again under his attention, daring to believe this time would be different. She wanted to get used to the closeness she felt with him. She wanted to share her burden and lean on his strength. She just had to find the strength to cross the invisible line she'd drawn through the years.

That afternoon proved to be a slow one, but Grant wasn't surprised. Homecoming Weekend was a big celebration in Greer and most of the people had already started celebrating yesterday. Since his aunt had left to help the Booster Club, Sarah, finished with her work in back, sat behind the front counter ready to answer the phone or greet a non-existent customer.

At 3:30, he emerged from his office, his lab coat slung over his arm, a small medical supply box in his hand containing the kitten Sarah rescued that morning. Since the feline would be the only animal at the clinic that weekend, Grant decided to take it home with him. It would make the frequent feedings a lot easier. "I doubt we'll see anyone else today. Ready to leave?"

Sarah nodded. "You bet. It's beautiful outside. Since it's quit raining, I thought Rocky could use a little exercise in the park with his new toy." At the mention of his name, Rocky's tail thudded on the floor beside her.

"Great, I'll take you." But at the park, Grant didn't

drop Sarah off like he'd intended. Somewhere along the tree-lined streets, he decided there would never be a better time to talk to Sarah about what he hoped would be their future.

He parked and accompanied her to a secluded area within a group of oak trees, near a man-made lake. No one lingered in the peaceful surroundings, and he suspected they were all getting ready for the game that evening. "Nice spot." He whistled under his breath. "Imagine living here your entire life and not really taking full advantage of what it has to offer." Settling on a park bench, he patted to the spot next to him in hopes that Sarah would join him.

She did, after she retrieved a tennis ball from her backpack, unleashed Rocky, and threw it for him to fetch. "I can't imagine living anywhere more than a few years, much less a lifetime." Her sigh spoke volumes.

Gently, he placed his arm around her shoulders and drew her close. Her lack of resistance encouraged him as he pulled her closer and cradled his chin on top of her head, inhaling the sweet scent of her. Sarah. The tough, street-wise kid who, deep down, was just a scared and lonely woman, had wormed her way into his life and his heart.

Rocky returned with the ball, dropped to his haunches and gnawed away at the felt. Grant knew he should stop him, but he needed to talk to Sarah while he had the chance. "Sarah, about your job at the clinic . . ." He hesitated, not sure how she'd react to his suggestion.

She peered up at him, her green eyes widening in alarm. "No. It's not that. You've done a great job. You're a natural. I think, no, I know you'd make a great technician. Have you thought about . . ." The words jumbled in his brain as he tried to put them in a cohesive sentence.

His heart, his struggling practice, and his entire life would be committed. He loved her. He thought he'd fallen in love before, but he'd been wrong. He'd fallen in love with the idea of love, but those feelings were nothing compared to the deep, earth-shaking response he felt toward Sarah. It rocked him to the core.

He hadn't felt this tongue-tied since he'd asked Marla Stevens to the Homecoming Dance in ninth grade. Taking a deep breath, he started again. "What I'm trying to say is would you consider going to tech school? There's a good one in Denton that has an opening next semester. We can work out the tuition in trade, and when you're done, we can talk about a permanent fulltime position."

He hoped she would accept his suggestion—accept him.

Stunned, Sarah gripped the wood bench for support. A technician? A chance to work with animals as a career? Grant had just offered her the opportunity of a lifetime. Not only in the physical sense of providing a way for her to go to tech school, but in an emotional one as well.

He was like Mickey, Rocky's manager, in her favorite movie. He really believed in her and was giving her the chance to succeed in life.

The walls around Sarah's heart tumbled down. She had no doubt about her feelings for him now. She loved him even after she'd sworn never to allow anyone near her again after her childhood experiences. Yet in the time she'd worked for him, he'd shown her another side of family life and the meaning of unconditional love.

All she had to do was accept his offering. But in order to do that, she had to come clean with her past and tell him the truth. The whole truth. He believed in her, now she had to believe in him. And believe that he wouldn't judge her for what she'd done to survive on the streets. "Grant, I—I'm—I don't know what to say."

"Say yes." He gave her another searching look that sent shockwaves through her. A new Sarah emerged. One ready to release the past and fight for the future.

"Yes. But there's some things you should know—"

"I know everything I need to."

He lifted her chin and drew her face within mere centimeters of his own. Sarah felt herself drowning in his deep blue eyes as a slight breeze rustled through the leaves overhead. Using the pad of his thumb, he caressed her cheek, then slanted his mouth over hers.

Her heart skipped as she closed her eyes, anticipating his kiss.

Chapter Ten

Warm and inviting, Grant's caress turned her blood to a molten liquid as it sped through her veins. Timidly, she reached out and wrapped her arms around his neck like she'd seen countless others do. The idea didn't seem so foreign now. She inhaled, unused to such tender caresses, unused to being touched at all, but enjoying it just the same.

With Grant, she felt safe, protected, wanted.

She returned his kiss, which invited him to deepen the embrace. The sensations made her feel lightheaded and dizzy. But she didn't want him to stop. She didn't want him to ever stop. She had never known how it really felt like to be cherished, and even though he'd never said the word, she felt loved.

For too long she felt nothing, and now she felt

everything. Grant chased away the emptiness, the loneliness in her life, and Sarah thought she would die of sheer pleasure. Her heart sang in rapid staccato with his as the final walls around her heart crumbled to the ground.

Setting foot in Greer had been the best thing she'd ever done. Not only to make her life better, but because she'd found Grant. The one man who seemed to understand her, and accept her.

"I love you."

The words tumbled out of her mouth before she could stop them. Not that she wanted to because they were true, even if he didn't feel the same.

Grant ended the kiss as Sarah's words hit him like a ton of bricks. For one, he thought he'd never hear them. For another, they were in the park where any Tom, Dick or Harry could see them kiss. What had he been thinking? Or had he been thinking at all? His sanity had taken flight the minute their lips touched.

He could have hit himself for making such a public display of affection. That had not been his intention. She deserved better from him. "I'm sorry. That shouldn't have happened."

As she dropped her arms to her sides, Grant sat back on the bench and looked at her. Her skin was still flushed, her breathing shallow, but it was the expression on her face; wounded, haunted, and what looked like a sheen of moisture crept under her eyelids that made him feel like the worst kind of cad. His mother would have his hide if she found out.

"You're right, that shouldn't have happened," she whispered in a resigned tone.

He sensed her withdrawal immediately and could have hit himself again at the insensitivity of his words. She'd declared her love for him, which had taken him completely by surprise, but like an idiot he said the first thing that sprang to his mind and all he did was hurt her again. He knew those words had not been easy for her to say.

"Sarah. Look at me. It's not what you think." Gently he cupped her chin and forced her to look into his eyes. While he spoke, his thumb caressed the soft skin on her jaw. "I love you too, sweetheart. Don't think that we're finished. We're not. Let me rephrase my statement. I'm not saying it shouldn't have happened, just not here. We need to be in a more private place."

Grant watched as her lips softened into a smile and beckoned him again. He leaned down and took possession of them for a mere second, tasting her. He wasn't worthy of her. As he rose to his feet, he reached out his hand to help Sarah off the bench.

"Come on. We can continue this at my place after the game."

"What game?"

Grant released her, bent over, picked up the ball, and threw it past a waiting Rocky, who gamely ran after it, his tail flying out behind him.

"It's Homecoming Weekend at Greer High School. The football game is tonight. Lindsay is on the cheerleading squad and Jeremy plays the trumpet in the band. If I don't show up, Aunt Mildred will have my head for breakfast."

"We certainly don't want to disappoint Aunt Mildred," Sarah agreed. "She's way too kind."

"Okay then. Let's grab a quick bite to eat, then go see the game. Then afterwards . . ." He pulled her to him again and gave her a kiss filled with promise of things to come. Heck, it was all he could do not to finish what he'd started, even if they were in the park. "If we don't leave now, we'll never make it."

"Bummer."

He swatted her on her bottom playfully. "Come on, it'll be fun. My family will be there; you've already met most of them, and maybe a few of my old high school buddies.

"Fine." She gave him a smile. "At least this time, I know what to expect. I think. C'mon, boy." As she put the soggy, half-chewed ball back into her backpack, Grant leashed Rocky, and they headed for the van.

"I'd grab a jacket," Grant suggested as he pulled up outside her apartment. "The game usually lasts for a couple of hours, and the nights can get pretty chilly when you're standing outside."

"Okay, stay here. Give me a few minutes to change clothes and feed Rocky."

Out of necessity, Sarah had made him remain in the car as she and Rocky bounded up the three flights of stairs to her apartment. With her body still charged and her emotions still raw from the kisses, she didn't want to take any chances that they'd be late to the game. Although if she'd had her way, they wouldn't be going at all, but she didn't want to upset Grant's Aunt Mildred either. She liked the matriarch of the Morrison family.

It took only five minutes for Sarah to exchange her blouse for a sexy, pale yellow, form-fitting sweater, and give Rocky one last kiss on his wet nose before putting him in the kennel with a few treats. Then she joined Grant, her oversized jacket slung over her arm as she exited the main door of the apartment building.

"Red?"

"Is something wrong with it?" She looked at him perplexed. Grant wore a look of horror as she jumped in the passenger seat and closed the door.

"Yeah."

Sarah froze. What had she done now? Had she chosen a color he hated? Even though she loved him, she realized there was so much she didn't know about him. "What's the matter? I don't have another jacket."

A twinkle suddenly appeared in his eyes. "Relax, Sarah, it's only the opposing team's color. Greer takes these things seriously. I'd get shot if I let you wear that tonight, no matter how much it compliments your hair. I have something at home that will work. You don't mind, do you?"

Sarah relaxed immediately, glad it was something trivial. "No. Not at all. We wouldn't want to upset the whole town now would we?" She winked, knowing they both remembered the kiss in the park. What would the good citizens of Greer think if they found their upstanding vet in a lip lock with a girl with a shady past? That thought sobered Sarah. How would Grant or his family react, if they ever found out the truth?

Sarah had tried to tell Grant, but he said he knew everything he needed to know. Maybe he did. Maybe it didn't really matter after all. Maybe all these years she'd been harboring false expectations of how people would react.

They drove in silence for a few minutes as they entered a part of town where Sarah had never been before. Not that she'd ever really had time to explore Greer. Still she liked the quiet, tranquil atmosphere. Or maybe it was the man beside her.

Out of the corner of her eye, she studied him. The way the dark hair on his arms added depth to the muscles underneath his tan skin sent her pulses swimming. And the way the fading light of day softened his chiseled features disrupted her breathing. It was all she could do not to reach out and touch him. Touch his generosity, caress his patience, stroke his humanity. And know that for just this space of time he was hers.

A wave of contentment coursed through her as the endless possibilities drifted through her consciousness—a career, a home, maybe even a family like the one in the poster on the wall of the clinic. It might have taken awhile, but the dreams she dreamed of when she was a child seemed about to come true. She didn't ever want to leave Greer or Grant or Rocky. She loved them all.

Sarah woke from her thoughts as Grant pulled off the main street onto a side street and into a maze of houses on the left, town homes on the right. "Come on in a second. I'll introduce you to the rest of my family."

On the front porch, he handed her the box with the tiny kitten she'd rescued earlier. "Here, hold kitty for a second while I contain the brood." The sound of excited barking reached her ears as he opened the door. Two dogs, both brown and black with specks of white fur, ran to meet them. They jumped up on Sarah, sniffing her intently.

She laughed, petting their heads one at a time. "They must smell Rocky."

"This is Max and Matilda." He roughed up the fur behind their ears, then ushered them to the back door so they could run outside and do their business. "The yard is fenced," he assured her as three auspicious-looking cats came around the corner and took their turn curling themselves around Grant's legs. "And these are Florry, Jasper, and Boots. Hello kids, you've got a new roommate for the weekend."

Grabbing the box from her, he knelt down and let the resident cats sniff at the little fluff of orange fur. Sarah laughed as the big black and white one regarded Grant intently, and the gray one lifted his head and padded away. The calico one seemed to be the only one to like the kitten and began licking it all over.

"I think that one likes her."

"Florry likes everything. She's even been known to try and nurse the things Boots and Jasper catch in the yard, don't you girl?" He scratched the cat under the chin before rising and setting the box on the kitchen table to his right, then leaned over and picked up the black cat with the white paws. "Your turn next. Boots likes the girls, here. Hold him." Grant plopped Boots in her arms.

Sarah almost dropped him. The cat was far heavier than he looked. Readjusting his position, she carried him as she followed Grant outside. The cat purred his agreement and tried to knead her shoulder with his paws.

"Ouch. I'm not a pin cushion," Sarah chastised him gently. The indignant look on his face made her squeeze him. She hoped the cat she rescued that morning grew up to be just as big and as self-indulgent as Boots.

A cool gust of wind blew wisps of hair across her

face. She shivered, glad Grant was going to let her borrow a jacket. The temperature had dropped since the sun set.

"Come here Max and Matilda," Grant urged, clapping his hands. In the light from the porch, Sarah could see his dogs chasing each other around.

Sarah laughed. "I'm glad to see your dogs listen about as well as Rocky."

"I don't always listen to myself either." Grant gave her a look that curled her toes. Sarah's mouth went dry at the promise of things to come. She clutched the cat so tightly Boots struggled and launched himself from her and dropped with a thud to the wood floor. With a displeased swish of his tail, he marched into the house.

"I thought we had to go to the game."

"We do." Chagrin crossed his features. "Come on. Over here we have Floppy and Peter." He walked to a cage off to the side on the back porch where two white rabbits with red eyes stared back at her.

"Peter Rabbit. How cute."

"My second cousin, Emily, picked out that name. You met her at the barbecue." He whistled to the dogs, who, tired of playing, ran past him inside. "After you." He followed her back into the house. "And over there is Jane Austen."

"What is it?" Sarah eyed the silver-and-black animal with the long nose and beady eyes curled up on the couch, not quite sure she liked the look of it.

"A ferret. A very pregnant one too, that's why she looks odd this evening." Grant walked over to the couch and patted the animal's head. "Are you ready to deliver Jane? Please wait until tomorrow, okay?"

With a precision that comes with practice, he placed food and fresh water out for his brood, then checked on the kitten. "I fed her in the van at your place so she'll be okay until we get back, but I'd better put her in the bathroom until proper introductions can be made to the rest of the gang. I think our friend here has had enough trauma today."

"They won't hurt her, will they?"

As Grant picked up the box, Sarah watched him scratch the kitten's head. A satisfied meow answered him back. Warmth curled through her again. Her boss genuinely cared about those around him, both human and animal. Her love for him deepened.

"Not as long as they're introduced correctly, but we don't have the time right now. I'll be right back."

After Grant disappeared up the flight of stairs that Sarah presumed led to the bedrooms, she checked out her surroundings and liked what she saw. The front hallway they'd come through earlier led to a spacious living area off to the right, and a warm, open kitchen and dining area to her left.

Off-white walls met polished-wood floors covered with colorful throw rugs that gave out a very homey feeling. As did the trees stationed by the windows and the plants that lined a shelf above the large-screen television. Sarah felt right at home.

The comfortable-looking practical furniture, covered with equally practical dark-blue fabric, invited her to sit down to wait. The masculine feeling in his house was softened by lacey white curtains and numerous pictures and odds and ends. Courtesy of the women in Grant's life no doubt. A fierce longing to become one of those women refused to leave, even after Grant returned.

"Ready?" He gave her a smile that intensified her desire for him.

"Yes."

He escorted her to the front hall closet, where he pulled out a purple-and-gold letter jacket and placed it around her shoulders.

"Here. This should keep you warm and in the right spirit tonight." She snuggled into it, inhaling Grant's scent and feeling his touch as if it were his arms, not the jacket sleeves wrapped around her. She couldn't wait until later.

"But what about you? What will you wear?"

"Don't worry." He reached in the closet and pulled out an almost identical jacket. "I have two. Both my parents and grandparents bought me one when I lettered in baseball in high school." He shrugged it over his broad shoulders and leaned down to kiss her lips. "Let's go or we'll miss more than the kickoff."

Dinner comprised of another pizza from Tony's.

And like everyone else dressed in some sort of purple and gold, they hurried through their meal. The place emptied out as the start of the game approached, and Grant and Sarah left with the tide.

As Grant maneuvered his van into one of the last open spots in the parking lot and walked around to help her out, anticipation crackled in the air. Sarah had never been to a football game, but she knew what she was about to experience had little to do with what would happen on the field. It would be her experience in the stands as part of Grant's family, and part of the community of Greer who had welcomed her without a question.

"Come on, we'll miss the national anthem." Grant grabbed her hand. At the front gate, he released his grip only long enough to buy her a program and a pair of the purple-and-gold pompoms sold by the Booster Club before they entered the stadium packed full of fans wearing purple and gold. Sarah was glad Grant had loaned her his jacket since it did appear that red was the opposing team's color.

The entire Morrison clan sat in their own cheering section, led by Aunt Mildred dressed completely in purple. "Glad to see you again, child. Grant needs to bring you around more often." She poked him with her cane. "Now come and give your old auntie a kiss."

Sarah said her hellos to all of the various members of the family as they wove their way through feet, purses and thermos bottles to the middle of the family section.

"Look, there she is." Sarah waved to Lindsay, who stood in the middle of seven other girls dressed in a purple-and-gold pleated skirt and purple sweater with a gold letter G on the front. Lindsay shook a pompom back at her before turning her attention to the field.

The game was confusing to Sarah, even with Grant patiently explaining the rules, but it didn't take long for her to figure out every time a player in the team colors advanced the ball that she should cheer. Just as loud and crazily as the rest of them.

Among the chattering crowd, the grunts and groans from the field, the constant cheering from the cheerleaders and the band, Sarah never felt so happy. She was completely surrounded by Grant and his warm and loving family. She squeezed his hand, which had never left hers since they sat down.

As Jeremy and the marching band took the field at halftime, Grant offered Sarah a mug of hot chocolate from Aunt Mildred's thermos. She accepted graciously, taking a cautious gulp, not sure how hot the liquid would be. A light flavor of peppermint surprised her.

"Don't drink it too fast," Grant warned her. "It's got schnapps in it."

"Isn't that kind of illegal at a game like this?"

"Don't tell Aunt Mildred."

They shared a smile as the second half started, and

continued enjoying their secret as the game came to an end. Greer scored the needed field goal in the last few seconds to put its team two points ahead. A cheer went up from the crowd.

"We won." Sarah, caught up in the fever, waved her pompoms furiously as the Greer High team exited the field. Grant hugged her around the middle, picked her up off her feet, and twirled her around.

"You know what this means, don't you?"

Sarah shook her head, laughing. "I have no clue. All I do know is I'm getting dizzier by the second."

As Grant set her on her feet, her laughter died in her throat. She swallowed at Grant's searching look.

"It's a tradition at Greer High to kiss the one you're with when the home team wins the Homecoming game."

Tenderly, Grand cradled her face between his gloved hands and leaned down. His mouth barely grazed the corners of her mouth. "You don't mind do you?"

"And upset tradition?" She melted into him, a tiny sigh escaping before he captured her lips between his.

The noise, the crowds, the world ceased to exist.

She felt complete, as if her life had meaning. The last of any doubts and insecurities fled, chased away by the man who had taken time to understand her, appreciate her. She lifted her arms and wrapped them around his neck and pulled him closer.

She'd been waiting for this moment, ever since

she'd met him that first day. She just hadn't known it. Those other kisses were simply a prelude, a warmup to the desire welling inside her. Even the kiss in the park this afternoon waned in comparison.

Sarah pulled off Grant's hat to feel the rich texture of his curly hair beneath her fingers. What started out as an innocent victory kiss, deepened into something exhilarating, even magical as she opened her mouth to let Grant explore its depths. Tongues mated in a ritual dance only the two of them heard the music to, while their bodies intertwined to the beating of each other's hearts. Later couldn't come soon enough.

"Hey, you two, come up for air." An amused voice she didn't recognize filtered in through her conscious. "I'm not sure we want to start a new tradition here."

They broke apart immediately.

Sarah inhaled sharply and stiffened when she saw the speaker's identity—a uniformed sheriff's deputy. That meant trouble. Never in all her experience with cops had they ever stopped by to have an innocent conversation. Her stomach lurched as the words tumbled out of her mouth before she could stop them.

"What have I done now?"

Chapter Eleven

Grant knew instantly that something was wrong. It had nothing to do with the kiss, and everything to do with the man standing next to them.

He sensed Sarah's mounting tension the longer the silence stretched. He'd suspected she'd had a few run-ins with the law, but her statement and reaction confirmed it. From the way the color fled her already pale skin, he knew it probably wasn't anything petty either. A rock formed in the pit of his gut, but he put his arm around her shoulders and cradled her close. "Hi, Joe. How are you?"

"Fine. You?"

"Likewise." At Joe's questioning look, Grant knew introductions were in order. "Have you met Sarah yet?"

He shook his head. "No, I haven't, but your sister's mentioned her. Hi, nice to meet you. I'm Joe. Gillian's boyfriend." Joe extended his hand toward her.

With a hesitant smile, she shook it. "I'm Sarah. Sarah Churchill." Sarah's stance became more rigid, and Grant could see her fighting for control. She lost the battle. Suddenly, she swayed, her voice wavering as she turned her head to look up at him. "Grant, I'm tired. Could you please take me home."

A look passed between Grant and Joe. A knowing look. Aunt Mary's request probably hadn't been off-base from the looks of things. He should have looked into her past himself like he'd intended, but he'd been in denial. Grant had no doubt he'd find some sort of rap sheet waiting on his desk first thing in the morning.

"Hey Joe, just getting off work? We're having a gathering at our place," Richard announced, oblivious to the tension around him. "Why don't you all stop by for a while?"

Grant looked at Sarah. She avoided his gaze, but he noticed some of the color had returned to her cheeks. He guessed it was more from the crisp air than anything else. "We'll pass, if that's okay. Sarah's got to work tomorrow."

Still on her guard, Sarah hardly spoke a word as he said their good-byes to the remaining family and friends. The night that had held so much promise was ruined. He knew it, and he knew Sarah knew it.

The drive home was a long, silent one.

At her apartment, the quick kiss he'd planned, deepened into another soul-searching, earth-shattering response. It left him breathless and his hands itching to explore Sarah's body, her background be damned. But he couldn't—at least not tonight.

"Goodnight, Sarah. I'll see you later."

Sarah slipped into the diner through the back door Saturday morning, hoping no one would notice her tardiness. She'd overslept, having spent most of the night tossing and turning, finally falling into a restless sleep around four.

Like a continuous tape, yesterday's events looped around in her head: the park, the game, and everything in between. Her heart ached for Grant, and she longed to feel his arms around her, filling her with warmth and driving away her loneliness, unhappiness, and fears.

For a moment, her dreams had come true. She'd belonged somewhere, to someone. She'd been loved. Until she'd blown it when she saw the sheriff's deputy. The sight of him set her on edge. Her years on the streets taught her to be wary of people in uniform. Any runaway or homeless person could tell a story about trouble with the law. Sarah included.

She'd hoped those days were behind her. Obviously, they weren't. Both Grant and Joe picked up on her reaction, she'd seen the look pass between them.

Now it would only be a matter of time before it all came crashing down.

Sarah cursed herself for her foolishness. She couldn't escape her past no matter how hard she tried. It would always be there, in black and white, on the police report.

A report that Joe could print out at any time.

Why hadn't she told Grant the truth? He'd given her plenty of opportunity, but her fear of opening up to anyone—even the one person who had genuinely seemed to care about her—had stopped her. Indecision chased her as she thought about the best way to tell him. She had to, and she had to make him understand before he found out from Joe.

Sarah wanted to scream. She wanted to fill her lungs and let out all the guilt, frustration and anger into the loudest sound she could make. She wanted to pull out her hair, break a glass, or pound her fist into the wall to relieve the pressure, but she didn't. She shut down her emotions just like she'd always done and concentrated on her opening duties.

As she hung her backpack in the employee section, she noticed the silence in the kitchen. Ted wasn't in his usual spot behind the line banging pots and pans around as he did the daily prep work, and Mabel was nowhere to be seen.

One glance around the tidy kitchen and she knew they wouldn't be opening on time. Odd. It wasn't like her boss to be so unprepared for the day. Something was up.

Fumbling to tie her apron over her uniform, she started toward the dining room. The sound of voices stopped her in her tracks as she placed her hand on the swinging door.

"She's got a police record? I don't believe it, Ted." Mabel sounded tired and weak, unlike her normal energetic, robust self. Sarah's arm dropped to her side, her feet frozen in place on the worn linoleum. Through the tiny window, she could see the owner and cook, and the other waitress sitting at the counter. They didn't notice her. "Who told you such a story?" the older woman continued.

"Joe Castle, the sheriff's deputy, caught me on the way in this morning."

"I don't understand. Why did he tell you?"

"Probably because she works here." The sound of the metal coffee spoon striking the side of the cup sent a chill down her spine. Ted sighed. "She lied on her application. I suppose I'll have to let her go when she comes in."

"Poor thing. She was such a nice girl. A good employee too. I can't believe it. And to think we'd taken her in and accepted her. Grant's family too. What's this world coming to? Well, we'd better get to work if we want to open today. I'll call Veronica." Sarah heard the sound of a stool scraping against the floor. "Does Grant know?"

"I don't think he did, but Joe was on his way to Gillian's. I'm sure he'll find out soon enough."

Too soon. Sarah wasn't prepared. As she staggered backwards, her hip connected with one of the stainless steel prep counters by the sink. She stifled the cry.

The floor wobbled beneath her and she grabbed onto the cool surface of the counter. Her whole world crashing down had happened sooner than expected. Her past had finally caught up with her. The mistakes she'd made had come back to haunt her. She'd been kidding herself she could forget.

Since coming to Greer, she thought she'd discovered a piece of herself that was missing, but she'd been mistaken. Lorraine was wrong. He did care about her past. Grant and his family would never accept her. Nor would anyone in Greer. She couldn't live with the looks and the stares. She'd had enough of that growing up.

Her dreams were shattered, her mind in complete chaos. A family, a home, a career. Things she'd longed a lifetime for, things she thought she'd finally found, things she now knew would be forever out of her reach.

Her world had spun out of control again, and this time it hurt worse than the first time, because this time she allowed it to happen. When she'd been a child, her parents' deaths had ended the illusion of a family, even if it was a dysfunctional one. From there, she'd been cast adrift by the system, always on the outside looking in.

Wanting what she couldn't have.

Wanting to belong.

With Grant and his family, she'd managed to reach out and feel it, for a fleeting second. Nothing more. Her pride wouldn't allow her to remain. Forcing her feet to move, she ran to the employee area, grabbed her backpack and escaped out the back door.

Rocky greeted her at the clinic with his usual affection, jumping up and licking her face, even though she'd been gone only fifteen minutes. Sarah hugged him as tears streamed down her cheeks. "Rocky, I've been such a fool."

Even though she'd taken him for a walk earlier, she took him for another one, simply for the memories. Grabbing the blue leash, she hooked it to his collar. Since she still used the same set Grant had given her that first night she gave Rocky a bath, the image of Grant surfaced again. More tears stung at the back of her lids. For someone unused to showing emotions, Sarah had done a complete turn around. All because of Grant.

The fresh air did little for her mood. Running away again was not the answer, but it was the only thing she knew to do. Sobbing, she let herself back into the clinic.

Rocky had never done anything to her but show unconditional love and here she was abandoning him again, as did his previous owners. She knew better than to take her dog with her when she had no idea where she was going herself. Grant would just have to find him another home.

Her heart wrenched in two, but she had no one to blame but herself. She'd allowed herself to open up to Grant. She'd allowed him to tear down the walls around her heart. She'd allowed herself to love him.

With Rocky at her side, she walked around the office, and memorized every detail from the stain on the white linoleum floor in the reception area, to the poster of the happy family on the wall. While Rocky was a far cry from that dog in the poster, she'd almost begun to imagine the three of them superimposed over the models' images. Even down to the house with the white picket fence and a big backyard.

Closing her eyes against the painful image, she walked into Grant's office and settled into his leather chair. She could still feel the imprint of his body carved into the seat and smell his scent, mingled with the tangy spice of leather.

Hurriedly, she retreated to the back room. "Good-bye, Rocky." She let out a wail and hugged her dog one last time before she stood and let herself out the same way she came in. "Just remember that I'll always love you. You too, Grant. Especially you," she added softly under her breath.

* * *

Gillian met him at his condo as he came back from his morning jog. One look at her face told him more than the paper she held in her hands.

"Come inside. No need to entertain the neighbors."

His sister followed him to his study. "We got this early this morning. It's not too bad, but it's not great either, Grant." His sister sighed, the sound grating on his nerves. "Joe thought it would be better if I explained everything, but if you have any questions, he's at home."

The stress that started in his neck muscles last night returned with renewed vengeance and zapped any energy he'd managed to muster. His run was a distant memory. Grant rubbed the palms of his hands across his face to clear the sweat, then rubbed his hands on his shorts before he sat down. "Let me see."

Gillian handed him the paper and settled in one of the upholstered wingback chairs across from his small desk. "This is only her adult record. Anything she did as a juvenile would be sealed."

With trepidation, Grant stared at the surprisingly short list. As far as he could tell, she'd only had one infraction but it was a big one—breaking and entering, trespassing, and arson. Bile rose in his throat at the last word. Arson. Sarah didn't look the type. Not that he would know what an arsonist looked like.

He'd always thought they'd be some deranged person with a vendetta, carrying around a can of gasoline and a match. But he realized they could look like the average Joe, or in his case, the beautiful Sarah. Just a few years ago, not far from Greer, in the Bakersfield and LA area, one of the fire departments' own had caused a string of fires for some reason that wasn't really important to Grant.

Somehow, he couldn't imagine Sarah doing any of the things documented here. The black images blurred on the white sheet of paper as her image wavered in his mind's eye. Her tentative smile, the light dusting of freckles that graced her face, her curly red hair and her curvaceous body beckoned him.

God help him, he loved her.

After setting the paper on his desk, Grant pinched the bridge of his nose with his forefingers. Shoulders slumped, he exhaled sharply. "I don't believe it, Gillian. There has to be some mistake. Sarah's not the type."

He heard Gillian rise and round the desk. She put her hands on his shoulders and began to massage. Her fingers felt good, easing some of the tension, but he wished it was Sarah, not his sister who stood behind him.

"I'm as upset as you are, Grant, believe it or not, I liked her. So she may not look like the type, but this report doesn't lie. How do we know what she's done that's not on this paper? How do we know she hasn't graduated to being . . . being a con artist?"

The chair had grown uncomfortably hard. Grant shifted, but found no relief so he pushed himself out of his seat and paced the confines of the small room. Realization slashed at his insides as the final pieces of the puzzle that he'd assembled during his jog fit together.

Sarah had lied to protect herself, not to hurt him.

Grant continued pacing even though his study was too small. Every third step he had to turn around and go the opposite direction, but he couldn't stop. Sarah and the impact she had on his life were too important.

"This isn't one of your high-budget movie scripts. She tried to tell me about her past and I blew it off. And I know she's not a con artist. Sarah never asked for a thing. In fact, she refused my help from the beginning. Everything I did, I did because I wanted to. I wanted to help her. I took more from her than she ever took from me."

"You bet you did." Aunt Mildred, her snow-white hair still in curlers from her early morning appointment at the beauty shop, stormed through his door, followed by his mother, two aunts, and his two sisters, Patty and Caroline. "You're full of hogwash, Gillian, suggesting that sweet child's a con artist. That girl's no more a thief than these fake boobs built in my bra." With that, his aunt patted herself on her chest.

Startled by his family's sudden appearance, Grant slumped back into his chair. "Good morning, Aunt Mildred."

"Same to you. Now let me see that so called report." His aunt's gnarled hands snatched the paper from his grasp before she sat down. Silence fell on the room as they all waited for her response. "This incident happened over seven years ago."

"She was never convicted either," Gillian responded quietly. "The charges were dropped before the case went to trial. It's kind of hard to gather from the wording, but Joe's assured me it's true. Right now, he's trying to get in touch with a friend who works in the Bay area to see if he can find out what happened."

"This is what you dragged me out of Lynette's Beauty Parlor for? Who here doesn't have something they're *not* ashamed of. Why, Grant, seems to me I remember an incident about some toilet paper and Coach Jackson's house? And what about all those 'For Sale' signs? And Gillian, getting caught drinking alcohol on prom night, with the mayor's son, no less. Carolyn, we won't even go there."

His aunt stomped her wood cane on the floor. "And you," she pointed her bony finger at Aunt Mary, "I'm sure you're involved in this somewhere. Don't give me that I-don't-know-what-you're-talking-about look. And don't think I don't know about the time you snuck out your window to go cavorting with that good-for-nothing Bill Baxter."

"You're right, as always." Grant smiled as he remembered the time he and his friends had childishly taken a jumbo package of toilet paper rolls and decorated his coach's house because he'd been benched for a playoff game.

With reason. He'd been caught red-handed smoking a cigarette before practice senior year. His first and last cigarette. "Seven years ago, Sarah had been only a year older than me when I did that. Everyone makes mistakes."

Hope coursed through him. Realization dawned that the Sarah Churchill written about in this report was not the same Sarah Churchill who walked in off the streets and into his life, just as he was not the same person who toilet–papered Coach Jackson's house. He'd stake his life on it.

Grant retrieved the paper, crumpled it in his hands, and threw it toward the wastebasket. It missed, which didn't surprise him since he'd never been much of a basketball player. As the ball of paper came to a rest on the floor, everything became clear for him.

"I don't care what happened. I love her, her past be damned. I'll do everything to convince her to be my wife."

Love? Love.

He'd fallen for her the moment she'd stepped through the clinic doors carrying an injured Rocky. He'd trusted her then, and trusted her now. He trusted her with his business, his life and his heart.

Whatever she'd done, she'd done out of necessity. Not too many people would understand. No wonder she kept running. But until she faced her problems head-on, she'd just keep running. A knot formed in his stomach. He couldn't let that happen.

"Good. I'm glad you finally realized that," his aunt said. She smiled then rose from her chair. "I'd begun to think you'd never get married. Come along, girls. After my hair is done, we have an engagement party to plan. How exciting. When are you going to tell her?"

"Now." Grant rose from his seat and ushered the women of his family out the door. He had no time to waste. "After you, ladies."

Grant jumped in his van, jammed it into reverse, and quickly backed out of his garage. He just missed hitting his neighbor's car as he careened into the street. With an apologetic wave, he sped off, trying to keep within the posted speed limit.

Greer's Diner was located on the other side of town, not too far from the clinic, or Sarah's apartment. At least 6 stoplights away from him—6 long, red stoplights. Slamming on the brakes, he barely stopped in time from entering the intersection. Fortunately, at this time of morning, traffic was light, or he might have caused an accident. He'd never seen such a quick yellow signal.

He hit the steering wheel in frustration when he realized he'd missed the timing sequence. Now he'd be stuck waiting for every light between him and Sarah. Each second that passed seemed like forever.

Drumming his fingers against the dashboard, his mood darkened. Tension built inside and out, weighing heavily on his shoulders. His stupidity had made his head overrule his heart. He'd probably ruined everything. Instead of fighting for her last night, he'd let her down, just when she'd needed him most—just as every other person had done in her past.

"Come on, change."

The light finally turned green.

Five minutes later, he pulled into the diner parking lot, his nerves wound tight, his mood uneasy. Slipping into the last vacant spot, he took a deep breath. He'd finally made it, but what was he going to say to Sarah?

Customers filled every table. "Hi, Grant," Veronica hurried past him, her arms loaded with plates of food. Over the din, Grant could hear Mabel calling out an order to Ted. Scanning the small area, he saw many familiar faces, but not the one he wanted to see.

The tightness that had started in his midsection, spread to the rest of his body. He caught Veronica on her way to the coffee machine. "Hey, Veronica. Where's Sarah?"

"Dunno. She never came in today. There's an empty stool at the counter if you want to eat. Be right there," she hollered to a male patron sitting in a booth by the window.

His gut feeling had been right. Sarah was gone.

And with her departure, his heart.

Chapter Twelve

Grant slammed the door shut behind him as he entered the clinic. After the shock of Sarah's disappearance wore off, his anger had set in. Not at her, but at himself.

His reaction last night had been no better than the people who had taken her in when she was a child. Instead of reaching out to her, comforting her in her need, he'd pulled back.

Banging his fist against the wall, he left a hole in the drywall. The contact sent a jolt of pain up his arm, but that was nothing compared to the pain in his heart, or what Sarah must be feeling. He'd seen the wounded look in her eyes last night as he dropped her off at her apartment—all because of him. She'd brought a ray of sunlight to his life and he'd blown it.

And she'd left him.

An empty feeling coursed through him thinking about her, and how far she'd come since she'd first walked through the clinic doors. Sarah. Alone, vulnerable, and hurt, somewhere in central California, since he was sure she was not in Greer anymore. The only question was, where did she go? The gnawing sensation in his stomach worked its way to his heart.

He needed her back.

Switching on the lights, he glanced around. Stark white walls stared vacantly back at him. He sighed, his anger gone. Numbness spread through him. Somehow, the thought of continuing without her left him cold.

He hadn't really felt like opening today—he warred with himself over whether to open the clinic or search for Sarah—but he had obligations, and bills to pay. When he was finished with his two appointments, he'd tear the surrounding communities apart trying to find her.

As Grant walked down the hall, Rocky slunk toward him, his tail between his hind legs and his big brown eyes staring up at him woefully. Grant squatted to scratch him behind the ears. He wasn't the only one hurt by Sarah's defection.

"She left you too, huh boy?"

Rocky sighed and placed his head on Grant's knee. Touching the dog's nose, he found it warm and dry. Rocky was sick . . . heart-sick for Sarah. Just like him.

With one last pat, he rose to his feet, made a pot of coffee and headed toward his office. Rocky followed. The dog wouldn't leave his side, not that he could blame him. The place was empty, the life had disappeared with Sarah.

He settled himself behind his desk, and stared at the spiderweb in the corner of the ceiling, forgetting the mail and the rest of his tasks. He couldn't help but think of Sarah. Her laughter over the past few weeks filled his brain.

The woman who'd come into his life unexpectedly and turned it upside down with her silent strength and resilience. The memory of the first time she had stood outside the door. Bill in hand, Sarah had been uncertain, then defensive, then angry. He swore he could still feel the imprint of her finger on his chest where she'd poked him weeks ago. It amazed him how far she'd come in such a short time.

His cousin, Susan, was right. Sarah was like the azalea, just waiting for the right time to blossom. She'd started to. He needed to see that she finished. As soon as he found her.

Time was ticking by too fast. Sitting here, thinking about her didn't do him any good. He needed to act, but then again, canceling Mr. Ericson's appointment didn't do him any good either, since his business depended on repeat clients and their referrals.

Rocky nudged his hand, begging for another pet. Grant obliged, stroking the thick black fur. He loved her. Heck, they both loved her. And they needed her back. In a way, Grant could understand why Sarah left him, but he couldn't understand why she'd leave Rocky. Her dog had done nothing. Something wasn't right.

It all became clear as he began to scratch Rocky under the chin while looking into his eyes. Sarah had no choice. Leaving had probably killed her, just like the thought of Sarah spending a night or a week in a shelter until she got herself together, was killing him. But until he figured out where she'd gone, there was nothing he could do.

The bell sounded over the front door.

Grant looked at his watch. It was too early for his first appointment. Sarah? His heart beat faster in his chest as Rocky's ears raised, his attention on the soft sound of footsteps coming from the reception area. The dog let out a yelp and ran to the office door, only to return more forlorn than before, as Gillian stepped in.

"She's gone, isn't she?" Gillian asked.

Grant nodded. He should have known better than to get his hopes up when he'd heard the bell. Except for the first two days, Sarah had always used the back door.

"I'm sorry." His sister sat down, a genuine look of sorrow across her features. "Where do you suppose she went? Aunt Mildred will be disappointed. I suppose I should go tell her."

A vision flashed in his brain. The answer was so simple. "Don't tell Aunt Mildred anything yet." Reaching under his desk, Grant grabbed the phone book and plopped it on the wood surface. The noise startled Rocky, who jumped up and skittered from the room.

He flipped through the pages, finally finding the number he wanted. Cradling the receiver to his ear, he punched the buttons. "I haven't a clue where she went, but I think I know how she'll get there."

Sarah sat huddled in the back of the Greyhound, her two bags packed underneath the bus, heading toward Los Angeles. She'd left with no more than she'd arrived with, except the painful memories of Grant. After all these years, she thought she had learned that lesson. Obviously not. Love was conditional and nothing was free. Still, in spite of everything, she missed Grant and she missed Rocky.

Pain swelled in her heart as tears formed. Through the mist, she stared at the grease stain on her dress. In her haste, she'd forgotten she still wore her uniform. It wouldn't be the first time she'd been accused of stealing, but it would be her last. She'd send it back to Ted as soon as she settled down, and tried to forge a new life. Maybe in a big city, she could blend in.

"You look a little down, honey," the elderly woman in the seat next to her remarked as she set her knitting in her lap. She'd boarded at the last stop, but Sarah had ignored her, not ready to talk with anyone.

Maybe she should. "Is it that obvious?" She sighed and looked out at the passing scenery. The grass had dulled to brown and most of the trees had lost their leaves. The bare limbs reached out toward a dismal sky filled with gray clouds that threatened to spill rain any moment. The weather did little to lift her spirits.

"Running away never did any good." The needles clicked together as the woman began to knit again.

Sarah turned away from the window and regarded her carefully. She guessed her seatmate to be in her late 60s because of her frosted-white hair and the years of lines etched into her skin. "How did you know?"

She smiled at her as she looked over the rim of her glasses. "I was young once too, you know, and very much in love. Besides, I don't know of anyone who'd commute such a long distance to work in a restaurant."

"Oh." Sarah tried to pull her short jacket down to cover her uniform. "Who says I'm in love?"

"Take a look at yourself, child. It's written all over your face." She reached into her bag, pulled out a blue ball of yarn and carefully added it to the burgundy strand. "What happened?"

Three months ago, Sarah would have ignored the lady, but that was before Grant. Before his kindness and generosity had changed her and her views about herself and humanity. Even Rocky had helped her change by showing her the meaning of unconditional love.

Unconditional love. Maybe it existed for dogs, but it sure didn't extend to the people department. His kindness and generosity were probably a front too. She didn't know, she didn't have much experience to go on. It hurt to think that Grant was no better than the people who'd raised her. She sighed. She'd begun to believe he was different.

His kiss told her he was different. The look in his eyes last night told her another story. Her heart was breaking in two. Which was the real Grant?

"Don't want to talk about it? I understand. But if I had listened to anything but my heart, I wouldn't be as happy as I am today."

The woman leaned down and retrieved a small photo album from her bag and handed it to Sarah. "This was my husband, George." She pointed to the black and white photograph of them on their wedding day, standing in front of a courthouse.

"At first, I tried to run from my problems too. Our families were dead set against us getting married because of our religious differences. But soon, I realized they were all wrong. I loved George, and I was determined nothing would come between us—not our religions, not our families, nothing. I convinced him it was the right thing to do, and we eloped."

She turned the page where Sarah could see a photograph of her seatmate, George and two infants. "He gave me two children, Mary and George Jr. before he died in an automobile accident. And they gave me four grandchildren." She turned to the next page where Sarah could see the grown children with their spouses with two children apiece."

"I'm sorry about George."

"I'm not. We only had a few years, but he made me happy. I don't regret a thing, even if I had to fight for the family I wanted." She shut the book and returned it to her bag.

A real family. Something she dreamed of, even long before she met Grant. She just hadn't realized it. She thought she had found it with the Morrisons, but that was before her past and her fears came between them.

Or was that her excuse to distance herself from Grant?

Yes.

Sarah didn't like the answer and shredded the toilet tissue in her hands she'd retrieved from her backpack. Grant had always been there for her—even last night. He'd been shocked, but he'd had every right to be.

She was the one who'd blown everything out of proportion by letting her pride get in the way. She should have explained everything then. She should have made him understand about her past, about everything. She should have reached out to him. But no, all she'd done was retreat and let Grant think the worst of her. The war of emotions was written in his eyes and still she'd kept quiet. No wonder Grant dropped her off with hardly a word.

But his last kiss still lingered on her lips. He'd awakened her. She'd always shied away from emotional contact and support because she was afraid— afraid of rejection, afraid of the complications, afraid of feeling emotions. It had always been easier to rely on herself.

That wasn't what she wanted anymore.

She was tired of running, tired of her fears, and tired of not knowing her future. A future that would be lonely without Grant. As her thoughts skimmed over the days they'd spent together, everything became crystal clear.

She knew enough about him to believe that when he learned the truth about her record—another case of being blamed for something she didn't do—he would accept her. "I've been such a fool."

The woman gathered her in her arms and hugged her gently. "You're only human, child. Your situation may not be the same, but you're no different than I was at your age. Go back. Everything will be okay."

The bus pulled into the next stop. As her seatmate gathered her things, said good-bye and departed, Sarah sat paralyzed in her seat, staring out the window, her hands clenched into fists. She wanted to go back. She needed to go back. She needed to find the strength to quit running and get off the bus. Once she did, her fate, for better or worse, would be sealed. It was a chance she had to take.

And she didn't have much time.

All the passengers getting off had left, and she could hear the few people that had boarded, taking their seats. She took a deep breath. As her one hand grabbed the black strap of the backpack, her other hand grasped the top of the seat in front of her so she could propel herself to her feet.

"Excuse me, is this seat taken?" A familiar voice filtered through her thoughts. Sarah looked up and dropped her bag. The familiar voice came with a familiar face.

"Grant. What are you doing here? Rocky!"

"We're on our way to LA. What are you doing here?"

"Being a fool."

She flew into Grant's arms as he stood in the aisle, glad to feel his solid strength around her, comforting her. This was where she wanted to be, not alone in the back of the bus, heading toward an empty and lonely existence. Today had been the longest day of her life.

"No. I'm the fool. I'm so sorry, Sarah. I let you down last night."

"But—"

He silenced her protest with a kiss. A long, drawn out kiss that sent her pulses spinning and her heart racing. She reached up and wound her arms around his neck, pulling him closer, mindless of the fact they weren't alone.

"Sarah, my beautiful Sarah. You had us so worried." Grant cradled her face between his palms and began planting tiny kisses on her cheeks, her nose, and her chin.

Woof. Pushing Grant out of the way, her dog lunged for her. His warm wet tongue lapped at her hands, then the tears on her face, as his tail thudded excitedly against the seats.

"Rocky, down you bad boy." Sarah managed to push him down, even though he seemed to have grown bigger in just the few hours she'd been gone. She knelt to hug him, wondering how she could have even thought to leave her man, or her dog.

"What's this?" She felt something hard attached to his collar. Sarah parted his fur and spotted the black velvet box. Her heart leaped to her throat and her hands shook as she untied the ribbon that released it. She looked at Grant.

"Open it."

At his gentle prodding, she opened the lid to reveal a solitaire diamond. Tears sprang to her eyes as she eyed the simple, yet elegant ring. She looked at Grant and wondered how she could have ever doubted him. Love truly was unconditional and certainly free.

"Let me have it a second." He lifted it from the box and reached for her hand as he knelt in the aisle. She gasped as he put the ring on her third finger. "Come home, Sarah. I love you. Will you marry me?"

Happiness swelled inside her. Never in a million years did she ever think this was how it would end when she boarded the bus in the early morning hours. Grant was her hero, a fighter, her own Rocky. She could hear the imaginary chorus in her head as she threw her arms around him again and kissed him passionately.

"I think that's a yes," a man called out from the front of the bus.

Sarah ignored him as well as cheers and clapping erupted around them. She didn't want to let Grant go, even for the briefest time. She'd waited her whole life for this moment and was going to savor every single second. She whimpered as he pulled away.

"We'd better get off now, if you don't want a long walk back to the van," Grant murmured in her ear. "Besides, we've got some unfinished business to attend to, remember?" Sarah blushed as he placed his hand protectively on her arm and escorted her and Rocky off the bus and toward his waiting van.

The sun broke through the clouds overhead, bathing them in its warmth. Birds sang in the trees around them as they watched the bus pull away with a puff of diesel exhaust. Sarah waved happily, glad she'd finally stopped running, glad she'd finally be able to put her past to rest.

"I need to tell you what happened." Sarah slipped

her hand into his, then turned to face him. "The fire wasn't my fault. There were five of us. Homeless teens living in an abandoned warehouse. We lit the small fire to keep warm while we slept. It got out of control. Next thing we know the whole place was burning. I was the only one over eighteen, so I got the rap." She gave him a rueful smile. "At first, the owner was going to press charges, until he found out the situation. He dropped them because the building was going to be destroyed anyway. Of course, it still shows up on my record, but that's not everything—"

"And I stole a bunch of 'For Sale' signs and planted them in my geometry teacher's yard, which is a misdemeanor, if I'm not mistaken." Grant tucked a stray piece of hair behind her ear before brushing her cheek, then her lips with the tips of his fingers. Sarah closed her eyes, relishing his touch. "What I'm trying to say is I'm not perfect, Sarah, and I don't expect it of you either. I'm sure there's a lot of stupid things we both did that we'll have plenty of time to talk about because I want to know, and I want you to know everything . . . later."

Sarah leaned her head back and let out the loudest scream she could muster. As she released the air, she expelled all the pent up emotions that had been buried inside her for years. It felt great to be alive.

A startled Grant stared down at her.

She laughed. "Don't ask."

As she rested her head against his chest, a warm

and fuzzy feeling took hold of her. She never wanted it to end. "I love you too. And in answer to your earlier question, yes, I'll marry you." She gazed up at him and smiled. "Wow. I've never said that before, and I thought I never would. I've always shied away from emotional contact and support for fear of getting hurt. Until you. And to think, I'd almost given up the most precious things in my life. You, Rocky and my happiness."

"I wasn't about to let you."

He leaned down and sealed their pact with another long, drawn-out kiss. As Sarah reached under his shirt to feel the warmth of his skin, she couldn't wait to get back to his place to start what should have begun last night.

He stopped her roaming hands. "Wait. Your bags."

Sarah put her hand on his arm to keep him from jumping in the van and driving after the bus. "Don't worry, Grant. There's nothing I need in them anyway. Someone else is welcome to my past, I'm done with it, okay?" She kissed him lightly. "Now take me home."

After settling themselves in the van, Grant put it in drive and turned onto the highway that took them back toward Greer. Toward home. Sarah would never leave again. She leaned into the seat with Rocky's head resting on her lap, Grant's hand holding hers.

"Before our engagement party tonight, there's a house I want you to look at that's not too far from

Greer," Grant said, a smile on his lips. "It has a huge yard and a white picket fence. I think it would be perfect for a bunch of little Morrisons, three dogs, four cats, two rabbits, a pregnant ferret, and maybe a foster child or two."